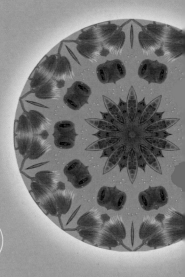

What parts of the front cover picture do you see in the design to the left?

How many star points can you count?

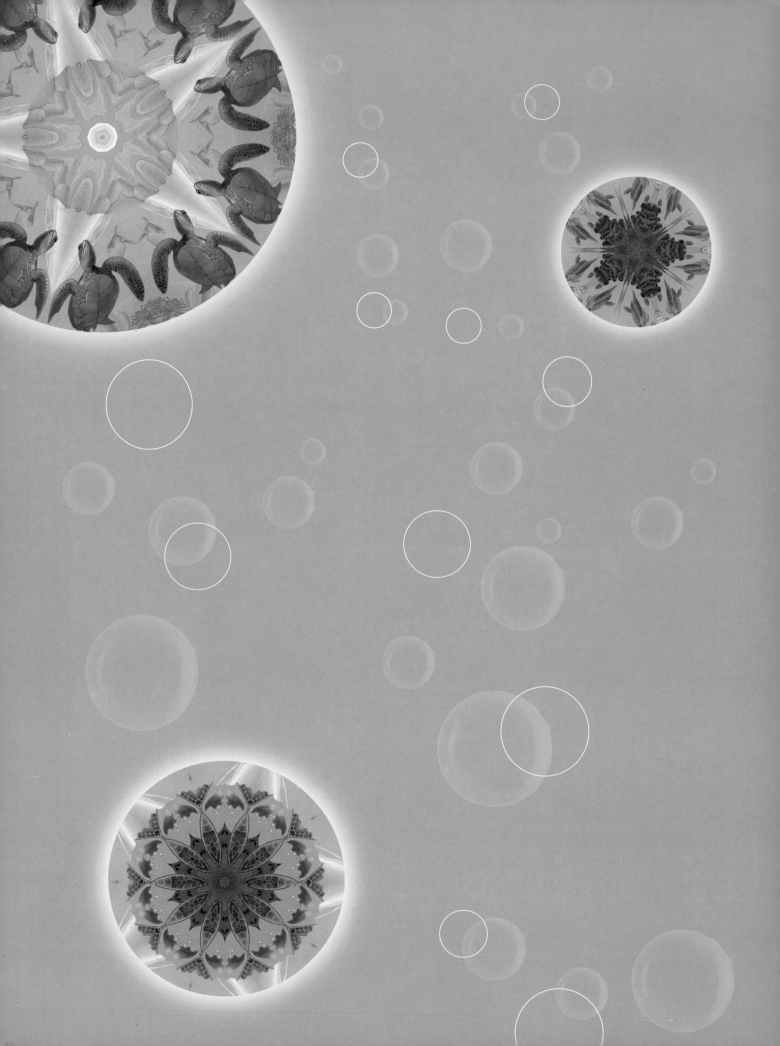

Literacy by Design™

Sourcebook
Volume 2

Program Authors

Linda Hoyt

Michael Opitz

Robert Marzano

Sharon Hill

Yvonne Freeman

David Freeman

Rigby®

A Harcourt Achieve Imprint

www.Rigby.com

1-800-531-5015

Welcome to Literacy by Design,
Where Reading Is...

Imagining

Thinking

Exploring

Literacy by Design: Sourcebook Volume 2
Grade 3

ISBN-13:   978-1-4189-4419-3
ISBN-10:   1-4189-4419-X

Printed in China
1 2 3 4 5 6 7 8   985 13 12 11 10 09 08 07 06

Discovering

Questioning

UNIT ▸ Taking Care of Business

THEME ⑨ From Factory to You
Pages 258–287

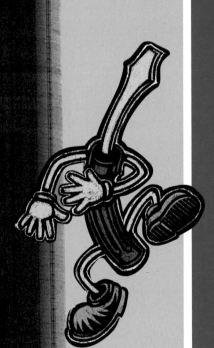

Modeled Reading

Shared Reading

Interactive Reading

THEME 10 Money Matters

Pages 288–317

v

UNIT Shoot for the *Stars*

THEME **11** **Our Solar System** Pages 320–349

Modeled Reading

Shared Reading

Interactive Reading

THEME 12 # Explorers in Space

Pages 350–379

UNIT We, the People

THEME **13** **Making Laws** Pages 382–411

THEME 14 **Every Vote Counts** Pages 412–441

PLACE BALLOTS HERE

UNIT Our Valuable Earth

THEME **16** # Recycle and Renew

Pages 474–503

Detroit Industry, North Wall, 1932–33
Diego Rivera (1886–1957)

THEME 9 From Factory to You

THEME 10 Money Matters

Viewing

This artwork is a fresco, a type of mural painting done on fresh plaster. Diego Rivera, a Mexican painter, created this mural for Henry Ford, of Ford Motor Company. It honors the American factory worker and celebrates Detroit's famous automobile industry.

1. What can you learn about a factory by looking at this fresco?

2. What kind of work do you think the people are doing in the painting? What clues helped you decide?

3. What do you think the factory sounds and feels like for the workers? What makes you think so?

4. How do you think the factory makes money to pay the workers?

In This UNIT

In this unit, you will read about how products are made. You will also read about money and learn ways to manage your money and use it wisely.

From Factory to You

Contents

Modeled Reading

Shared Reading

Interactive Reading

HOW IS PAPER MADE?

**by Isaac Asimov
and Elizabeth Kaplan**

Precise Listening

Precise listening means listening
for special word meanings.
Listen to the focus questions
your teacher will read to you.

From the Mill to Your Desk

We use paper every day. Books, notepads, boxes, tissue—it's all paper! Paper is made from tree pulp at factories called paper mills. Paper is cut at the mill. It is made into different products. Every **scrap** is used. Then the products are ready for **distribution**. They are loaded onto trucks and shipped out.

Soon the paper products arrive at a store where they will be sold. If people do not buy the products, the paper mill or other factory might **halt production**. That means it will stop making the product. Factories will make an **abundant** supply of paper products if people buy them. That is how the paper company earns money!

Paper Mill

Paper Rolls

Paper Products

Structured Vocabulary Discussion

Work with a partner to pick the vocabulary word that goes with each phrase below. Discuss your ideas.

Stop!

bits and pieces of items

making new clothes in a factory

more than enough

fruit traveling from a farm to stores

> Throughout the week, add to your vocabulary journal entries. Record new insights and other words that relate to this week's vocabulary.

Picture It

Copy this word wheel into your vocabulary journal. Name things that are **abundant**.

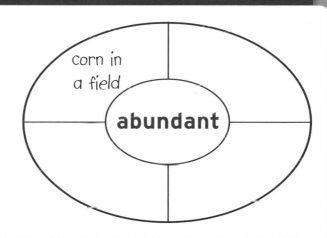

Copy this word organizer into your vocabulary journal. Fill in the chart with things that might help in the **distribution** of a product.

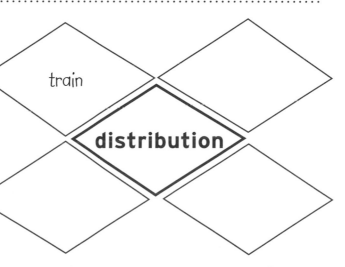

Make Connections
Compare/Contrast Information

When you **COMPARE** and **CONTRAST** information you show how things are similar and different.

Think about how things are similar and different as you read.

TURN AND TALK Listen as your teacher reads from *How is Paper Made?* and models how to compare and contrast information. Then, with a partner discuss answers to these questions.

• How are the two methods of making wood pulp similar?

• How are the two methods of making wood pulp different?

TAKE IT WITH YOU When you compare and contrast information, you see how things are similar or different. This helps you make connections to what you read. When you read other selections, make a chart like the one below to help you compare and contrast information.

Item 1 mechanical method

Item 2 chemical method

Differences

bark taken off logs

logs soaked into water

logs ground into tiny pieces

Similarities

both make paper

both take place in a factory

Differences

logs cut into wood chips

wood chips soaked in chemicals

wood chips cooked over high heat

A Loaf of Fun

by Ann Weil

It was warm inside the bus. Jacob pulled his sweatshirt over his head. His glasses slipped off his nose and skittered across the floor.

CRUNCH!

"Sorry," said Emily. She picked up the broken glasses and handed them to Jacob. Emily and Jacob were partners on this class trip to a bread factory. Each set of partners had to write a report about what they learned. But how was Jacob going to see the factory without his glasses?

"We're almost there!" Jacob said.

"How do you know?" asked Emily.

"Can't you smell that?" said Jacob.

"You're right," said Emily, "It smells like fresh bread right out of the oven."

Inside the factory, Jacob's class met their tour guide, Lois. She explained to the class the purpose of each machine in the factory. The first machine weighed the flour and loaded it into a mixer with water and yeast. The mixer made a whirring sound. Next, they saw a machine cutting the dough into pieces. The pieces of dough were moved to a warm area to rise.

"After the dough rises, it goes into the oven," said Lois. "After the bread cools, it is sliced and bagged.

"Can we taste the hot bread?" asked Emily.

Lois asked her helper to pass out slices of warm, delicious bread.

Jacob knew what he would write for his report. Even though he hadn't seen everything on the tour, he had smelled, heard, and tasted plenty.

Sour Treats Move West

You can find many things in the desert city of Las Vegas. You can find clear pools and green parks. You can find museums, zoos, and roller coasters. Until recently the one thing you couldn't find in Las Vegas was a pickle.

Pickles are very popular on the East Coast. Sandwiches come with pickles in many stores. One deli in New York City even holds a pickle-eating contest each year. Pickles used to be rare out West.

Now this is changing. One company from New Jersey decided to bring their pickles west. The owners opened a pickle factory in Las Vegas.

Now the company makes pickles for restaurants, stores, and markets. Workers there also give tours of their factory. Just don't mind the smell!

Nouns

Activity One

About Nouns

A *noun* is a word that names a person, place, or thing. The following words are all examples of nouns: *Angela*, *doctor*, *sister*, *airport*, *school*, *candle*, *deer*. As your teacher reads *Sour Treats Move West*, listen for nouns.

Nouns in Context

Together with a partner, read *Sour Treats Move West* to find nouns. List the words in three columns: nouns for people, nouns for places, and nouns for things.

Activity Two

Explore Words Together

Look at the nouns listed on the right. What other nouns do you think of when you read each one? With a partner, brainstorm at least two other nouns for each noun on the list. Compare your nouns with another partner team's.

paper	worker
meal	factory
New York City	movie

Activity Three

Explore Words in Writing

Write sentences about a kind of factory you would most like to visit and why. Exchange sentences with a partner. Have your partner circle all the nouns in your sentences.

Genre

Personal Narrative

How an Idea Became a TOY

by Meghan Murphy

As I was growing up, my father and grandfather always kept a supply of coiled, plastic mesh in our garage. My sister and brother used to play with the pieces. One day they realized the material was like a spring. They would wind up the mesh, and it would shoot out of their hand. It would go *Whoosh!* What fun they had! My sister and brother had made a new toy. We called it a "spring thing."

One day, when my sister Colleen was 12, she and her friends were playing with the spring thing. Everyone thought that the new springy toy was a lot of fun. My sister said, "I think people would buy these. We should sell them!"

Have you ever had an idea about a new toy? How is your idea similar to or different from the spring thing?

TOY Inventor

Meghan Murphy
1252 Toy Place Lane
Easton, Michigan 55252
555.622.5262

My parents agreed. That night, our family talked about starting a new company. That talk was the beginning of our toy company. Later, we found a site where we could build our factory.

How do you think the way Meghan made her toy into a product is similar to or different from the way other toys are made?

Today, we have two factories to make our toys. One factory has more than 200 workers!

Our toy is made out of plastic. We buy this material from other companies. Then our workers weave the plastic together. After this, a hot blade cuts the plastic. Each cut is the same so the toys will be the same size. The blade is so hot that it melts the plastic.

Sometimes we must search for plastic in a special color. One time, my sister thought we should make a neon blue toy. I thought it should be neon yellow. Our family voted on which color we should use. Everyone must work as a team to make the right product.

Spring Things

Toy Fair

Say Something Technique Take turns reading a section of text, covering it up, and then saying something about it to your partner. You may say any thought or idea that the text brings to your mind.

When I was 14, I went to an international toy fair. This fair brought lots of people from the toy industry together. I went to help my parents tell people about our toy.

One man at the fair, from China, had pens with foam toppers on them. I thought it would be neat to put a foam topper on our toy. What if the foam was in the shape of a funny face or a character? The toy would still be able to fly, but it would be even more fun!

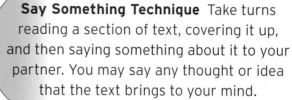

Name another toy product you have seen, read, or heard about. How is it different from Meghan's?

I had taken a Chinese language class at school. I knew that *wán jù* means toy in Chinese. So I decided to talk to the man about creating a new product. Soon his factory in China was making foam toppers for our toys. The toppers were shaped like different things such as a bee, a clown, and a fish. Our customers liked the new funny figure on top of our toy.

In high school, I took a business class. I learned that companies used surveys to help them decide what products they should make or what services they should offer.

A survey is a list of questions. I created a survey about our product. I asked my classmates questions such as, "What color and characters do you like best?" I also asked, "How much would you pay for the toy?"

The survey told us about a market for our new product. Markets are the people who might buy a product. Using this information, our company made other toys.

Our company creates a prototype for each new product. A prototype is a model of what the product will look like. We test the prototype with possible buyers. If buyers like it, we make the toy in our factory!

> In what ways do the *survey* and *prototype* help Meghan with her product?

Steps for Creating a New Toy

1. Use a survey to find out what kind of toy people want.

→

2. Use the answers to come up with a new toy idea for the market.

→

3. Create and test the prototype of the new toy.

→

4. Make the new toy in a factory.

Today, we sell our toys to schools, museums, and stores. If a company wants to have its name on our toy, we can make products just for them. The most unusual toy we ever made had a lion on top. We made it in a school's colors. The toy was a big hit. Once, we also made a hamburger toy for a restaurant. It looked silly!

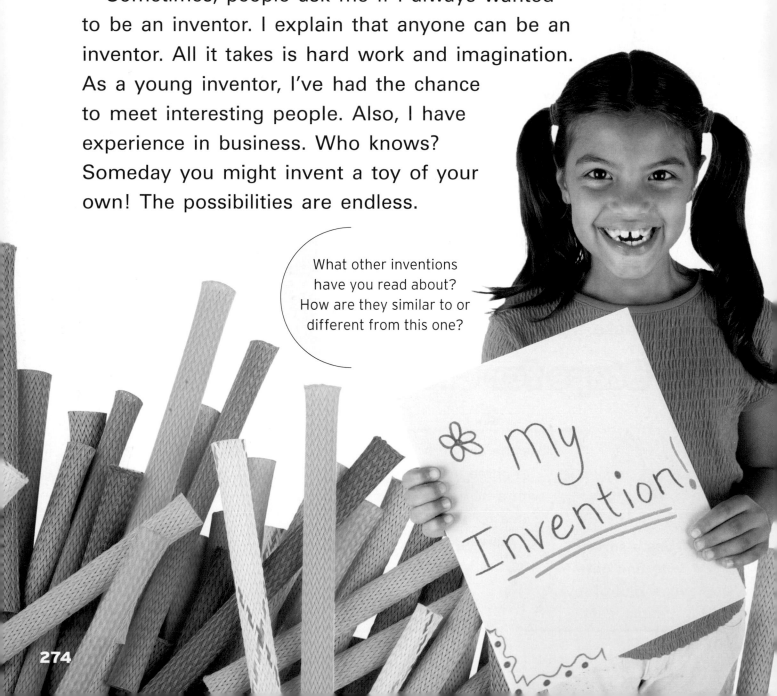

Toy Store

Sometimes, people ask me if I always wanted to be an inventor. I explain that anyone can be an inventor. All it takes is hard work and imagination. As a young inventor, I've had the chance to meet interesting people. Also, I have experience in business. Who knows? Someday you might invent a toy of your own! The possibilities are endless.

What other inventions have you read about? How are they similar to or different from this one?

Think and Respond

Reflect and Write

- You and your partner read *How an Idea Became a Toy* and said something to each other about each section. Discuss your thoughts and ideas with your partner.

- On one side of an index card write a connection you made with the text. On the other side, write how that connection compares and contrasts to the information in the selection.

Nouns in Context

Look through *How an Idea Became a Toy* for nouns. List the nouns you find. Choose ten of the nouns you found and write a paragraph about a toy you would like to make and sell.

Turn and Talk

MAKE CONNECTIONS: COMPARE/CONTRAST INFORMATION

Discuss with a partner what you have learned about how to compare and contrast information.

- How can comparing and contrasting information help you in your reading?

Discuss with a partner a toy that both of you enjoy. Compare and contrast that toy with the one that Meghan invented.

Critical Thinking

With a partner, list ways Meghan helped make her company successful. Then answer these questions.

- What could other companies learn from Meghan about making a successful new toy?

- What advice do you think Meghan would give to someone who wanted to make and sell a product for the first time?

What's *HOT* Today *Is Not* Tomorrow!

Gloria just *had* to have the *Starship* video game. The game was an **import** from China. It was the hottest game in the toy **industry**. Now every store at every **site** was sold out. Two local stores would order it. They wanted to charge an extra $20. Gloria also looked on the Web. The **scarcity** of the game had caused its price to rise.

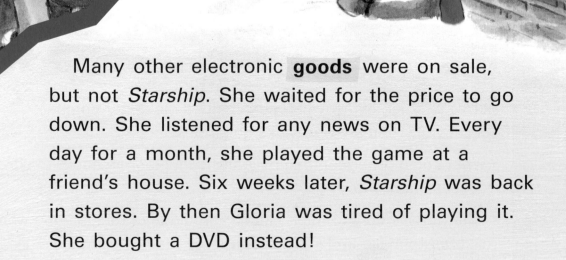

Many other electronic **goods** were on sale, but not *Starship*. She waited for the price to go down. She listened for any news on TV. Every day for a month, she played the game at a friend's house. Six weeks later, *Starship* was back in stores. By then Gloria was tired of playing it. She bought a DVD instead!

import   industry   scarcity   goods   site

Structured Vocabulary Discussion

Work with a partner to fill in the blanks with your new vocabulary words. Be ready to share your answers with the class and explain how the words in each sentence are related.

Fat is to *thin* as *plenty* is to _____.

Office is to *business* as *factory* is to _____.

A *house* is to *place* as *building* is to _____.

Eat is to *food* as *trade* is to _____.

> Throughout the week, add to your vocabulary journal entries. Record new insights and other words that relate to this week's vocabulary.

Picture It

Copy this word organizer into your vocabulary journal. Fill in the chart to tell what happens when there is a **scarcity**.

scarcity	People use something else

Copy this chart into your vocabulary journal. Fill in the columns with examples of **goods** each business provides.

	goods
dairy	milk, cheese, ice cream
hardware store	
sporting goods store	
deli	

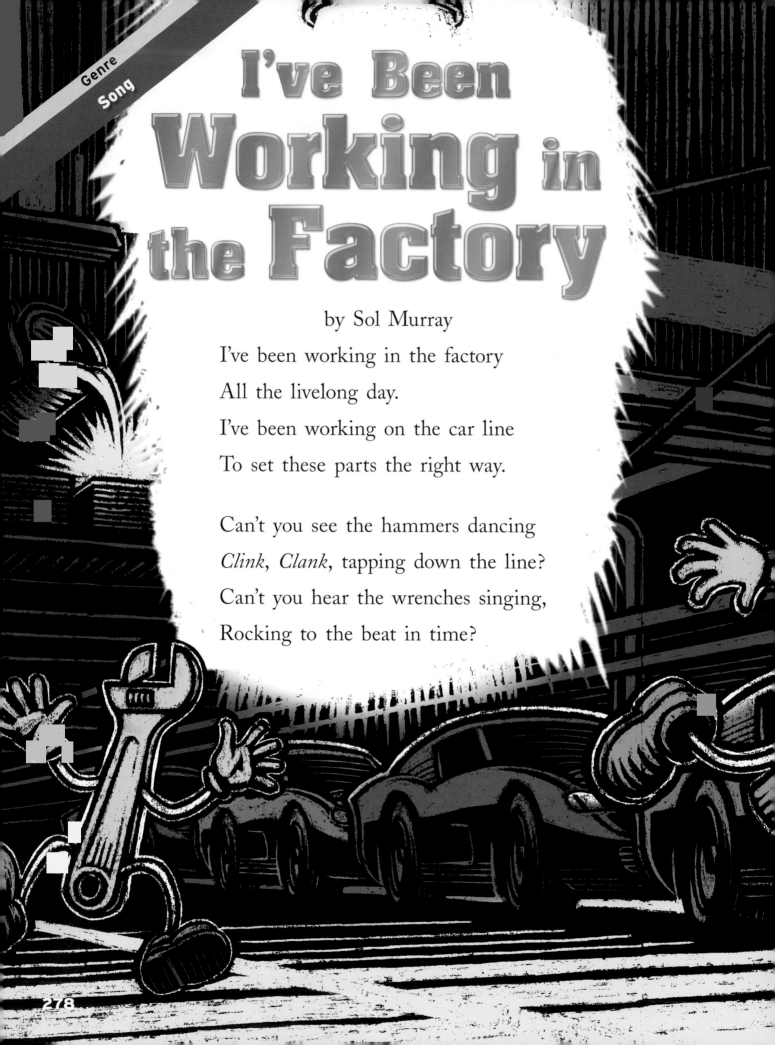

I've Been Working in the Factory

by Sol Murray

I've been working in the factory
All the livelong day.
I've been working on the car line
To set these parts the right way.

Can't you see the hammers dancing
Clink, Clank, tapping down the line?
Can't you hear the wrenches singing,
Rocking to the beat in time?

"I've got a special job, I've got a special job,"
The tools chant day by day.
"I've got a special job, I've got a special job.
And the car goes a-rolling on its way!"

We're working together in the factory,
We're working together with pride.
We're working together in the factory,
Making goods to travel far and wide.

Fee Fie Fiddle-ee-ii-o,
Fee Fie Fiddle-ee-ii-o-o-o-o,
Fee Fie Fiddle-ee-ii-o,
Making cars to travel far and wide!

THE Money Factory

Do you ever wonder where the change in your pocket came from? Money is made at the United States Mint. A mint is a factory that makes coins. The word *mint* used to mean "money" or "coin." In the United States, coins are made at mints in Philadelphia, West Point, Denver, and San Francisco.

Minting Machine

Many kinds of coins may be made at one mint. Most coins show famous people, such as President Lincoln on the penny. Others show buildings, such as the White House on the nickel. A mint makes coins in many sizes. It also makes coins from different metals such as copper and nickel.

Once new coins are made, they are stored in Federal Reserve Banks until they are needed. *Cha-ching*!

The Federal Reserve

Proper Nouns

Activity One

About Proper Nouns

A *proper noun* is a specific person, place, or thing. The first letter of a proper noun is capitalized. These are proper nouns: *Texas, Michelle, George Washington, Thanksgiving, Main Street, December.* As your teacher reads *The Money Factory*, listen carefully for words you think are proper nouns.

Proper Nouns in Context

With a partner, read *The Money Factory* and list the proper nouns. Identify each proper noun as a specific person, place, or thing. For example, the proper noun *Los Angeles* is a place, while *George Washington* is a person who was a president.

Activity Two

Explore Words Together

Work with a partner to write proper nouns related to each word on the right. Share and compare your list with other partner teams' lists.

countries	friends
singers	businesses
holidays	streets

Activity Three

Explore Words in Writing

Choose three proper nouns you listed in Activity Two. Write a sentence for each word you chose. If possible, add another proper noun to each sentence. Share your sentences with a partner.

My Cotton Dress

retold by Margaret Fetty

September 12, 1909

Dear Diary,

The "Wish Book" Catalog came today! It has many things to order through the mail. A person can buy a watch, a sewing machine, or even a typewriter!

I like to look at the ready-made dresses. I can't believe people can get dresses through the mail without making them at home or going to a dressmaker to be fitted! One pretty dress even has lace. The lace is an import from Ireland.

My dark, heavy dresses are not as dainty as the ones in the catalog. I asked Momma if I could order a new dress made from white cotton with lots of buttons. Momma said, "Your own dresses are nearly as good as new." She says if I still want the white dress when my birthday comes, we'll go ahead and get it.

Elizabeth

Elizabeth

> What important information do you learn on this page?

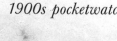

1900s pocketwatch

September 20, 1909

Dear Diary,

Papa has business up North. Momma and I are going with him. We started out last week.

Today we rode by a cotton field in Alabama. Women and children in the cotton field were bent over picking the cotton from the plants.

Momma told me that many families work together all day long under the hot sun to pick cotton. They must be done in by the end of the day. None of the children get to play. That does not sound like much fun to me!

I think I still want that white cotton dress from the catalog. It's as pretty as a picture!

Elizabeth

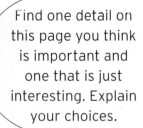

Cotton

Find one detail on this page you think is important and one that is just interesting. Explain your choices.

Early 20th century sewing machine.

Children in a cotton field carry bags of cotton that they have harvested.

283

**Read, Cover, Remember, Retell
Technique** With a partner, take turns reading
as much text as you can cover with your hand.
Then cover up what you read and retell the
information to your partner.

*Twelve-year-old worker
in a cotton factory*

September 24, 1909

Dear Diary,

Papa had to make a stop in Georgia. We
visited the Bibb Cotton Mill. This is where cotton
is made into yarn for clothing. I saw workers carry
in large cotton bales. The room was filled with
dust and dirt that the workers breathe in. Workers—called
"lappers"—smoothed the cotton into long sheets. A machine with
metal teeth cut the sheets into rope. The lappers must take care
so their hands and clothing do not get caught.

The cotton ropes then go to another
machine. Children walk along the floor all
day long. When a thread breaks, they
must quickly tie the ends together.

What do you think
is the most important
information on
this page?

Children work in the hot, dark factory
from seven in the morning until six at
night. They work to help their families pay for food and
housing. The children do not go to school. A ready-made
dress takes a great deal of work.

Elizabeth

*Workers weaving
cotton in a mill*

Spools of thread

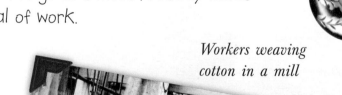

Early 20th century sewing materials

October 2, 1909

Dear Diary,

Yesterday, we visited the Everett Cotton Mill. A man named Mr. Miller gave us a tour. We went to the weaving room. It was filled with big looms. I had to shout to talk with Momma because of the noise. The cloth from this mill will be cut into dresses at another factory.

Today, we got to New York City. On the way to our hotel, Mother pointed out some wooden buildings. She said that people ate, slept, and sewed dresses in those buildings. Young girls help thread needles and sew buttons. They often work six days a week until nine o'clock at night! Because there is a scarcity of jobs, these people work for little money.

Elizabeth

> Do you think it is important to remember the name of the mill Elizabeth visited? Why or why not?

A family sewing clothes for which they are paid by the piece

Shell buttons

October 12, 1909

Dear Diary,

We all returned home today. I saw the "Wish Book" Catalog on my bed. I caught myself looking at the white cotton dress again. I thought about all the children who helped to make that dress. They work near dangerous machines. They do not make much money. Those children do not get to go to school and play like I do!

Momma asked me what I want for my birthday. I told her I do not want the white dress anymore. So instead we're fixing to have a big picnic with sweet tea and pecan pie. I am going to invite some children of the workers here in town. I was mighty sad about all the work they do to help make ready-made dresses. I'll be happier to play outside with my new friends at my birthday picnic!

Elizabeth

Do you think it is important to remember that these events took place almost 100 years ago? Why?

Early 20th century picnic

Think and Respond

Reflect and Write

- You and your partner read *My Cotton Dress* and retold the important information. Discuss your retellings.

- On one side of an index card, write details from one diary entry. On the other side of the card, explain why the details are important or just interesting. Discuss your choices with another partner team.

Proper Nouns in Context

Look for proper nouns in *My Cotton Dress*. Make three lists of the proper nouns you find: those that name people, those that name places, and those that name things. Write a short paragraph using all of the proper nouns that you found.

Turn and Talk

DETERMINE IMPORTANCE

Discuss with a partner what you have learned about how to determine importance as you read.

- Why is it useful to determine important and unimportant information?

- Look back at *My Cotton Dress*. Discuss with a partner the most important ideas or details to remember from this selection.

Critical Thinking

With a partner, brainstorm a list of important information about factories. Discuss the factories that Elizabeth visited in *My Cotton Dress*. Then discuss answers to these questions.

- What important information did you learn about the factories Elizabeth visited?

- Do you think children work in factories today? Why or why not?

- Why do you think people make rules and laws today to keep factory workers safe?

$ Dog $
$ Wash

Money Matters

Contents

Read Aloud

Shared Reading

Interactive Reading

MY ROWS AND PILES OF COINS

by Tololwa M. Mollel
illustrated by E. B. Lewis

Strategic Listening

Strategic listening means listening
to ask questions about the author's
purpose. Listen to the focus questions
your teacher will read to you.

LEARN TO EARN!

Do What You Like

Do you need a **strategy** to earn money? The answer is "Yes." If you have a plan, you can succeed. First, think about what you like to do. Turn it into a job! Decide how much money you want for **payment**. Then, ask your parents if your plan is OK. If they say "Yes," tell friends about your new idea.

Fresh Ideas!

You could make invitations for friends' parties. Wash or walk your neighbors' pets. Set up a lemonade stand. **Decorate** notebooks and sell them to classmates. You could ask if you can run an **errand** for a neighbor. Collect plastic bottles, glass, and cans and recycle them for extra **income**. Whatever job you choose, make sure it is something you enjoy!

strategy   decorate   income   payment   errand

Structured Vocabulary Discussion

When your teacher says a vocabulary word, your small group will take turns saying the first word that comes to mind. When your teacher says "Stop," the last person to say a word should explain how that word is related to the vocabulary word.

> Throughout the week, add to your vocabulary journal entries. Record new insights and other words that relate to this week's vocabulary.

Picture It

Copy this word web into your vocabulary journal. Fill in the circles with things you could **decorate** to sell.

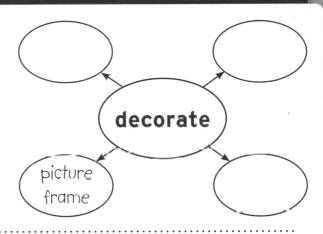

Copy this word organizer into your vocabulary journal. Fill in each rectangle with a kind of **errand** your family does.

293

Comprehension Strategy

Ask Questions
Author's Purpose

QUESTIONS can help you to understand why an author wrote something.

Ask questions about details in the text to understand why the author wrote it.

TURN AND TALK Listen as your teacher reads from *My Rows and Piles of Coins* and models how to ask questions to understand the author's purpose. Then discuss with a partner the answers to these questions.

• What do the details about the old coat and precious coins tell you about Saruni's feelings when he sets off into the crowd?

• Why do you think the author includes this information?

TAKE IT WITH YOU Asking questions about an author's purpose can help you understand a passage better. As you read other selections, ask questions to learn why the author wrote something. Then look for clues to help answer the questions. Use a chart like the one below to help.

In the Text	Questions That Help Me Think About the Author's Purpose
"'I must be the richest boy in the world,' I thought, feeling like a King. 'I can buy anything.'"	Why did the author describe how Saruni felt? Why did the author have Saruni say he was the richest boy in the world? Why did the author say Saruni could buy anything?

Based on the details, I think the author's purpose was to. . .

make the reader feel just as excited as Saruni is about having some money.

Watch Your Money... Grow!

by Jason Carpenter

Do you want to get the most from your money? Keep a money journal! You can use a money journal to make a *budget* and stick to it. A money journal will show you how you spend your money. Keeping a journal is also a good way to learn how to save your money. It will help you make plans for the future.

Write down all the money you earn or are given in your money journal. Keep a record of your *expenses* for any *items* you buy. Also, write down how much money you plan to save for an important goal or to *donate* to a charity.

Glossary

budget a money plan

donate to give, or contribute

expense an amount paid out

items things

Earn Money

Keep money in a safe place

Record what you earn

When you buy something get a receipt

Sales receipt
Snacks 1.75
total $1.75

Record what you spend

My Money Journal

Date	Income (allowance)	Expense
Nov. 3	$5.00	$.50 (gift for coach)
Nov. 4	_____	$1.75 (snacks)
Nov. 6	_____	$.75 (toy)

PIGGY BANK

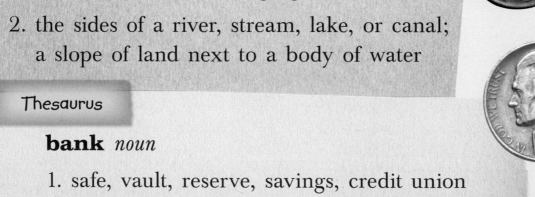

piggy bank

A container in which people keep and save money. The history of piggy banks goes back to the Middle Ages. During that time, people made all kinds of useful objects out of a clay called *pygg*. Potters made pygg dishes, cookware, and jars, and people stored coins in pygg containers. By the 1700s, potters began making pygg banks in the shape of pigs as a joke on the word.

bank (bangk) *noun*

1. a place where money is kept for saving, borrowing, and exchanging

2. the sides of a river, stream, lake, or canal; a slope of land next to a body of water

bank *noun*

1. safe, vault, reserve, savings, credit union

2. shore, cliff, coast, edge, waterfront, riverside

Reference Materials

Activity One

About Reference Materials

Reference materials are sources that provide information. You can use many sources to learn about different words and ideas. An *encyclopedia* gives information about different topics. A *dictionary* gives the meanings of words and also the pronunciations and parts of speech. A *thesaurus* lists the synonyms of words. Listen as your teacher reads *Piggy Bank* for the different kinds of information you hear.

Reference Materials in Context

With a partner, read *Piggy Bank*. Discuss the different information in each reference source. Describe to each other how you might use each reference source as you are reading.

Activity Two

Explore Words Together

money	cash
investment	quarter
savings	dollar

Work in a small group. Look up the words listed on the right using an encyclopedia, a dictionary, or a thesaurus. Meet with another group who used a different reference source. Discuss the information you found.

Activity Three

Explore Words in Writing

Choose a word or idea you would like to learn more about. Do research in one of the reference materials. Write a short paragraph on what you learned. Discuss with a partner why using different sources might be helpful.

The Wisest Wish OF ALL

retold by Lorraine Sintetos

It was a sunny Saturday, and all the Hoopers were busy. Dad was in his bike shop, humming. Mom was weeding her flower garden. Lucy, the oldest child, was painting wildflowers in a nearby field. She planned to look the flowers up in an encyclopedia and write a caption for each painting. Ben, the middle child, ran off carrying a bucket and a book on rocks. Nine-year-old Claire squatted quietly at the lily pond trying to catch a frog with her net. Suddenly, *Swoop*! Down came Claire's net.

"Hey!" cried a small frog, struggling in the net. "What's going on?"

Why do you think the author tells us details about each family member?

Claire had never met a talking frog before. "I'm taking you to a home I've made for you in my tub," she said.

"Oh, no!" snorted the frog. "Listen. Let me go, and I will grant you any wish!"

"Well I'd like a TV," replied Claire. "Mom and Dad don't think we need one."

"Hmmm. Your parents are probably right," said the frog. But he thought of a plan. He told her how to win a contest with a TV as a prize. Two weeks later, the Hoopers won a new TV.

Mom warned the family not to watch too much TV. But soon, the whole family was watching just about everything!

What important information does the author want you to know from this page?

One night, after seeing a car commercial, Dad said, "Our old station wagon runs well enough, but I want a big, new car like this one on TV."

The next day Dad went to the pond with Claire. They asked the frog for another wish. He promised to help.

Following the frog's directions, Dad found a new car on sale. He needed to borrow money from the bank to buy it. Then he had to get a second job to pay the bank.

Soon everyone else in the family wanted things. They all visited the frog at the pond.

Mom told the frog, "Our furniture is old. Our living room should look like the one on TV." The frog told her how to find a job doing computer work at home. This would help pay for the new furniture.

Reverse Think-Aloud Technique
Listen as your partner reads part of the text aloud. Choose a point in the text to stop your partner and ask what he or she is thinking about the text at that moment. Then switch roles with your partner.

How do you think the author wants you to feel about the Hoopers at this point in the story?

Another day, Lucy visited the pond. "Everyone has brand new clothes but me," she complained.

The frog told her of a babysitting job. There she could earn money for new clothes. At first she was excited to be working like her Mom and Dad. But she came home very tired.

Then Ben went to the frog. "Everyone else has a personal computer," Ben said. The frog told him of a job at an ice cream store in town. Soon, Ben's arms were sore from scooping ice cream all day.

The Hoopers' lives had changed. They were too tired to do anything but watch TV. One day the whole family went to the pond. They all spoke at once. "I want a bigger house . . . a trip to Hawaii . . . a motorbike . . . a horse!"

"Nonsense," the frog said. "What you really need is to be happy."

The Hoopers stared at one another in surprise.

"Why, yes!" exclaimed Mom. "I suppose we do."

What details or ideas on this page help you understand the author's purpose?

"Then take the new car back," the frog told them. "Stop working just to buy things you don't need. Enjoy your time together. Most importantly, TURN OFF THE TV!"

The Hoopers decided to follow his advice. They spent more time together and unplugged the TV. The three children returned to their outdoor activities and reference materials, and Dad hummed as he worked.

Claire visited the frog one last time. "Please, frog," she said, "will you grant my family one more wish?"

What do you think the author is saying to you about wishes and money in this fairy tale?

The frog looked doubtful, but he agreed.

"My wish," Claire said, "is that you don't grant us any more wishes!"

"That's the wisest wish I've heard!" croaked the frog happily. Then he dove off his lily pad.

Claire went off to photograph butterflies.

Think and Respond

Reflect and Write

- You and your partner have read *The Wisest Wish of All*. Discuss the thoughts and ideas you shared with each other.

- On one side of an index card, write a question you had about the author's purpose. On the other side, write an answer to the question.

Reference Materials in Context

Find unfamiliar words in *The Wisest Wish of All*. Use reference materials, such as an encyclopedia, dictionary, or thesaurus, to find out and write about the words. Share the information with a partner.

Turn and Talk

ASK QUESTIONS: AUTHOR'S PURPOSE

Discuss with a partner what you have learned so far about how to ask questions to understand an author's purpose.

- How can asking questions about the author's purpose help you as you read?

Look back at page 303. Discuss the clues on this page that help you figure out the author's purpose for writing. Share your ideas with a partner.

Critical Thinking

In a small group, discuss the changes in the Hooper family goes through in *The Wisest Wish of All*. Then answer these questions.

- Was the family better off before they met the frog? Why or why not?

- Why did the frog say Claire's last wish was the wisest wish of all?

Calling All Kids!

Are you 12 years old or younger? Join the "No **Fee** " Savings Club at Barton Bank and earn as you save.

Open a Savings Club account with as little as one dollar of your **personal** money. Every time you save $50, the bank teller will put an additional dollar in your account. That means if you save $100, you will have $102 in your account!

When you **invest** your money at the bank, you help people in your community. The bank lends money to people. This helps people pay for things they need. People **borrow** money to buy a house or a car, or to go to college.

Each month, the Savings Club newsletter helps you plan your **budget**. It will also offer new ways to save money.

Sign up now!

Structured Vocabulary Discussion

With a partner, finish each sentence to show what the vocabulary word means.

People *invest* their money so they . . .

If you have your own *personal* savings, you can . . .

When you *borrow* money, you should . . .

Throughout the week, add to your vocabulary journal entries. Record new insights and other words that relate to this week's vocabulary.

Picture It

Copy this word wheel into your vocabulary journal. Fill in the top half of the wheel with things you must pay a **fee** to do. Fill in the bottom half with things that you don't pay a **fee** to do.

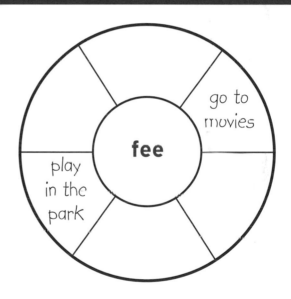

fee

go to movies

play in the park

Copy this word organizer into your vocabulary journal. Fill in the boxes with reasons you might make a **budget**.

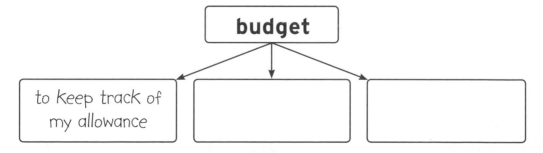

budget

to keep track of my allowance

When UNCLE BOB Came to Town

by Theodore Greenberg,

When rich Uncle Bob rolled into town,
our whole world turned upside down.
He showered us with presents and more still,
for my brother and me, a crisp $50 bill!

When Bob, in his fine suit, came into town,
our whole world turned upside down.
With the $50 we bought a chemistry set,
cool sunglasses, comics—and we weren't done yet!

When Bob drove his fancy car into our town,
our whole world turned upside down.
We bought new markers and stickers, a colorful kite to fly,
all of the things our parents couldn't buy!

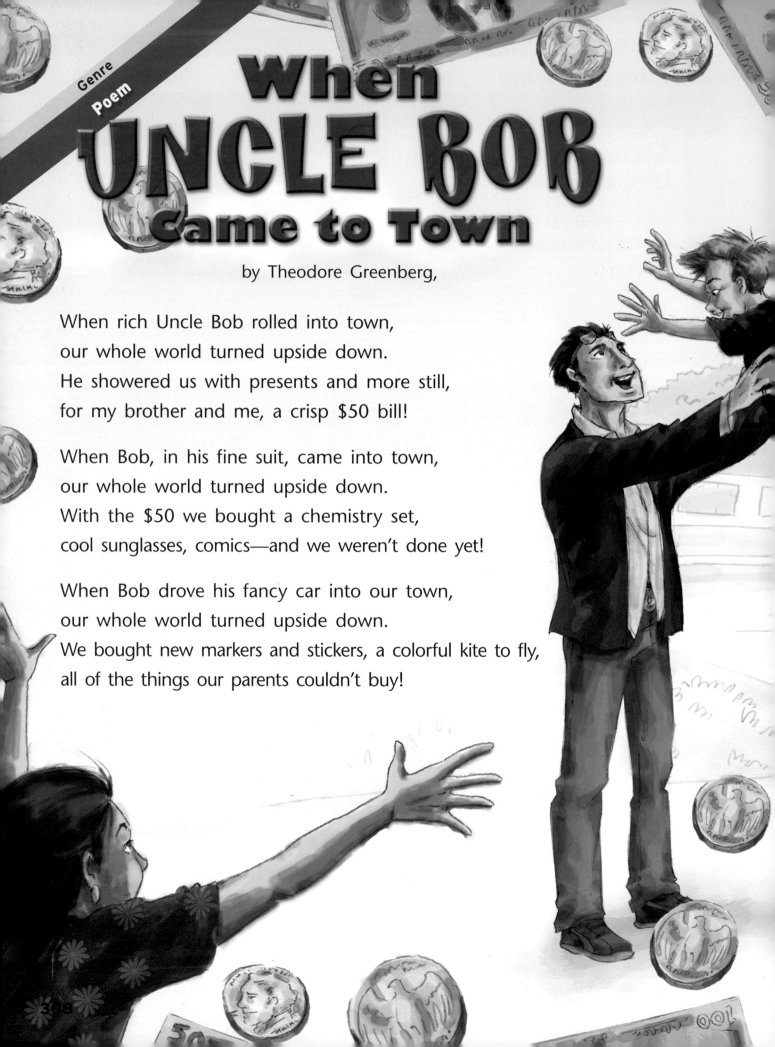

When our rich uncle waltzed into town,
our whole world turned upside down.
Once we decided to buy a new baseball.
But when we went to pay, we had no money at all!

We asked Uncle Bob to help us this one final time.
Could he spare a dollar, a quarter, one measly dime?
"Not this time!" he just laughed, "I can't spare a stitch.
My budget is quite tight now. That's how I stay rich!"

Money Matters

Ask B. Frank Lin!

Dear B. Frank Lin,

My best friend Sam and I need money for a school trip. Sam says we could mow lawns for money, but we would have to wait until spring to do that. I want to start a business by myself now, instead of waiting around. What do you think?

—*Patrick Penniless*

Dear Patrick,

As I always say, *Time is money*! Start earning on your own right away. If you wait, you will lose out. Remember: *The sleeping fox catches no chickens.*

Remember my other favorite saying, *A penny saved is a penny earned.* Put that money away for the future!

—*B. Frank Lin*

Action Verbs

Activity One

About Action Verbs

An action verb tells what someone or something does. The following words are all action verbs: *run*, *catch*, *laugh*, *break*, *ask*, *ski*, *drive*, *follow*, *borrow*. As you teacher reads *Ask B. Frank Lin!*, listen for action verbs.

Action Verbs in Context

With a partner, read *Ask B. Frank Lin!* aloud. Have your partner read one letter, and you the other. List all the action verbs you hear your partner read. Then, share your lists.

Activity Two

Explore Words Together

save	invest
spend	donate
count	plan

With a partner, list two action words related to each action verb on the right. Write several sentences, using as many of the words as possible from the two lists. Read your sentences to your partner.

Activity Three

Explore Words in Writing

With a partner, write three statements of advice about money, such as B. Frank Lin's *A penny saved is a penny earned*. Use a strong action verb in each statement you write. Share your work with another partner team.

Helping Others
ONE DOLLAR
AT A TIME by Susan Ripley

Imagine what you would do with $20 right now. You can probably think of lots of things! You might buy a toy, a book, or a T-shirt. You might go to the movies or invest your money with a bank. Did you ever think of giving your money away? When you use your money to help others, the good feeling you get can last a long time! You can help others with your money, one dollar at a time. Read on to find out how!

Have you heard of people who give their time or money to help others? Describe what you know.

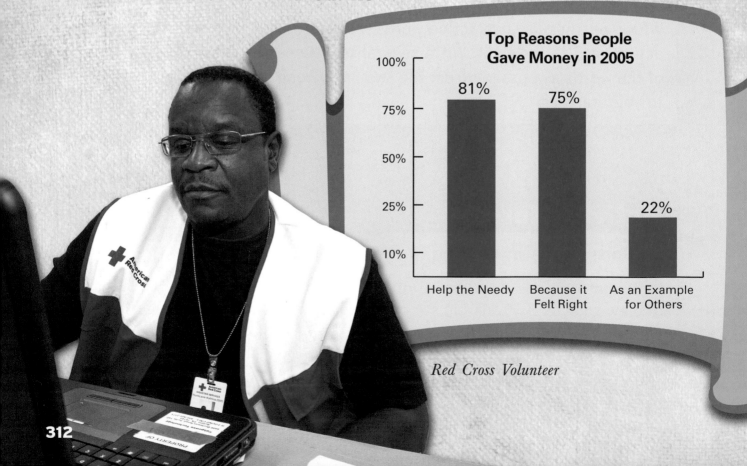

Top Reasons People Gave Money in 2005

100%
81%
75%
75%
50%
25%   22%
10%

Help the Needy | Because it Felt Right | As an Example for Others

Red Cross Volunteer

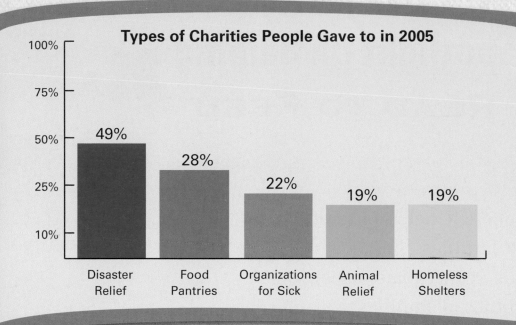

Types of Charities People Gave to in 2005

Category	Percentage
Disaster Relief	49%
Food Pantries	28%
Organizations for Sick	22%
Animal Relief	19%
Homeless Shelters	19%

THE BIG PICTURE: HOW YOU CAN HELP

How can I give money to others?

Find out about a charity you want to help. A charity is an organization that collects money to help others. It does not make a profit. Ask your family or talk to people in your community. Then work with an adult to send money to the right place.

> What is a charity that you have you heard about that helps people?

Why should I be careful when I give money?

Always ask an adult before giving money away. Sadly, some people only pretend to collect money for others. Most charities are honest and do important work.

How do I save money to give to others?

You can set aside some of your allowance or money you receive as a gift. For a charity, small amounts of money add up quickly.

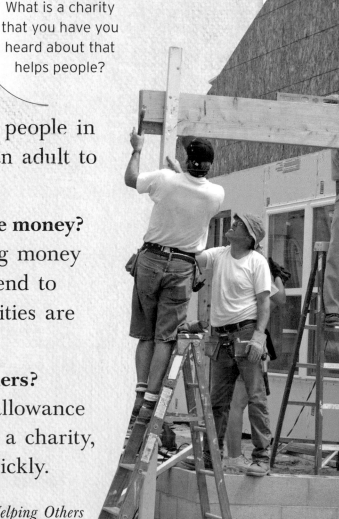

People Helping Others

313

Spotlight on Helping
READ TO FEED

What is *Read to Feed*?

The *Read to Feed* program works to end world hunger. It helps provide animals to needy families. The organization sends cows, goats, sheep, chickens, and rabbits to families all over the world. Each family cares for its animals. In return, the family gets things they need such as milk, eggs, meat, and wool. *Read to Feed* raises money to buy these animals.

How does *Read to Feed* raise money?

The people who contribute to *Read to Feed* are school children. Children watch a video and learn about needy families. As a class or school, they choose the animal gifts they will give. Next, they ask people to give money for each book read by a student. Then the school sends this money to *Read to Feed*.

Say Something Technique Take turns reading a section of text, covering it up, and then saying something about it to your partner. You may say any thought or idea that the text brings to your mind.

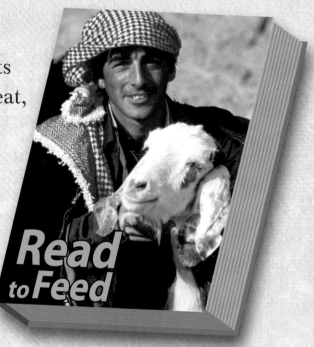

Bedouin Boy With Sheep

Do you know of a class or school that has helped raise money for a good cause? How is that school or class similar to or different from yours?

Spotlight on Helping
THE RAINFOREST ALLIANCE

What is *The Rainforest Alliance*?

The Rainforest Alliance works to save the rain forest. Rain forests have many things people and animals need. But rain forests around the world are getting smaller and smaller. Some people come and take plants and animals. Some use the land in ways that harm it. *The Rainforest Alliance* teaches people about rain forests. *The Rainforest Alliance* also encourages people to raise money for rain forests.

> Have you ever read or seen on television anything about rain forests? Explain.

How do people raise money for rain forests?

The Rainforest Alliance website gives many ideas for helping. You might have a contest or hold a yard sale to raise money. You could build a classroom rain forest and charge money for tours. *The Rainforest Alliance* uses the money it receives to help change how people use the rain forest.

A Rain Forest

Spotlight on Helping
ROOTS AND SHOOTS

What is *Roots and Shoots*?

Roots and Shoots is a group started by Dr. Jane Goodall. Dr. Goodall is a scientist and writer. She has worked with animals for many years. The group teaches people about the many dangers to animals. It offers ways to help.

Have you read in other books or magazines about Dr. Goodall's work? What is important about her work with *Roots and Shoots*?

What are some ways people raise money for *Roots and Shoots*?

People raise money for *Roots and Shoots* in many ways. If you want to help, you might have a fundrasier at school. You could hold an entertaining event, such as a concert or talent show, and charge a fee to attend.

Now you know about a few charities that help others. Would you like to help one of them? Or is there another cause you believe in? No matter what charity you give money to, you will be sure to feel good about it for a long, long time!

Dr. Jane Goodall and Friend

Think and Respond

Reflect and Write

- You and your partner have read and said something about *Helping Others, One Dollar at a Time*. Discuss with your partner your thoughts and ideas.

- On one side of an index card, write a connection you could make between the selection and another book or article you have read. On the other side, write how the two texts are similar or different.

Action Verbs in Context

Search through *Helping People, One Dollar at a Time* to find action verbs. List the words as you find them. Then use at least five of the verbs in a paragraph about how you can save and spend money.

Turn and Talk

MAKE CONNECTIONS: COMPARE AND CONTRAST

Discuss with a partner what you have learned about making connections by comparing and contrasting information.

- Why is it helpful to compare and contrast information in the stories and articles you read?

Look back at the sections on *Read to Feed* and *Roots and Shoots* in *Helping Others, One Dollar at a Time*. With a partner, list ways in which these two charities are similar and different.

Critical Thinking

With a partner, talk about how you feel when you give money or do something to help other people. Together, brainstorm a list of programs in your community that might need your help. Then answer these questions:

- How could you raise money for one of the programs?

- In what other ways could you help?

***The Starry Night,** 1889*
Vincent van Gogh (1853–1890)

Shoot for the Stars

Viewing

The artist who painted this picture was Vincent van Gogh. He wanted to create a special feeling about starlight at night. He painted the picture in 1889, the year before he died.

1. Do you think the swirls in the painting look like real starlight? Why or why not?

2. Does this painting look like a real night sky? Why or why not?

3. What feeling about the night sky do you think the artist was expressing when he drew the swirls in the painting?

4. This artwork was painted before people or spacecraft traveled into space. How do you think people at that time found out about objects in space?

In This UNIT

In this unit, you will read about the planets in our solar system. You will also read about how people explore space to help us learn more about the solar system.

Contents

Our Solar System

Modeled Reading

Shared Reading

Interactive Reading

The Solar System

by Dana Meachen Rau

Critical Listening

Critical listening means listening to compare and contrast ideas in the selection. Listen to the focus questions your teacher will read to you.

The Hubble Space Telescope

Our Eyes to the Universe

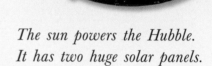

The sun powers the Hubble. It has two huge solar panels.

The Hubble Space Telescope was launched in 1990. This powerful **telescope** works much like a regular telescope. The Hubble telescope orbits high above Earth's atmosphere. It allows us to **perceive** objects in space more clearly.

From Earth, a planet or star appears as a **speck** in the sky. The Hubble telescope allows us to see up close a **crater** on a planet's surface or stars billions of light years away. The Hubble has taken pictures of each **planet** in our solar system. It may even discover a new planet!

The Hubble gives us a much closer look at stars like this one.

Structured Vocabulary Discussion

Work with a partner to answer the following questions about the vocabulary words. Explain your answers.

Does a *crater* look more like a pit or a hill?

Can a *speck* be a lump of coal or a grain of sand?

Would you use a *telescope* to see Venus or a baseball game?

Throughout the week, add to your vocabulary journal entries. Record new insights and other words that relate to this week's vocabulary.

Picture It

Copy this word web into your vocabulary journal. Write a word in each circle that has a similar meaning to **perceive**.

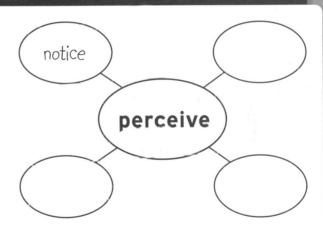

Copy this word organizer into your vocabulary journal. Give an example of a **planet** and describe it.

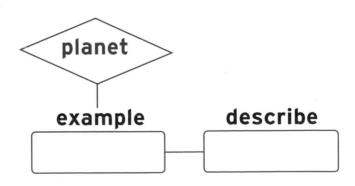

Infer
Conclusions

A **CONCLUSION** is a decision you make about what you read.

Combine what you have read with what you already know to draw a conclusion.

TURN AND TALK Listen as your teacher reads from *The Solar System* and models how to draw a conclusion. Discuss with a partner the answers to these questions.

- How many moons does Mars have?

- What other inner planet has a moon or moons?

- How many moons are in orbit around the inner planets?

TAKE IT WITH YOU When you draw conclusions, you are a reading detective. Clues from the text and information that you already know will lead you to a conclusion. As you read other selections, try to draw as many conclusions as you can. Use a chart like the one below to help you as you read.

In the Text		In My Head		My Conclusion
Mars is an inner planet and has two moons – Deimos and Phobos.	**+**	Earth is an inner planet and has one moon.	**=**	Three moons are in orbit around the inner planets.

HELLO, NEPTUNE!

by Ann Weil

Adir and his friend Dennis were going home from school when Adir saw something strange in a hole. He reached in and pulled out a bright, blue, round rock. A blue mist floated around it.

"Have you ever seen anything like *this*?" Adir asked Dennis as he showed him the rock.

Suddenly, an image of a boy appeared on the rock. The boy was blue. He was wearing a shiny silver suit. He had a long, rubbery neck and extra eyes on the ends of tentacles.

"Don't be afraid," said a friendly voice.

"Is the rock *talking*?" asked Dennis.

"What—I mean, *who* are you?" asked Adir.

"My name is not important," said the blue boy.
"I am glad you found my telecommunicator.
I will be there soon to pick it up."

"Your tele—what?" asked Adir. "Besides, you're
already here, aren't you?"

"Not exactly," said the blue boy. "I am on the
planet your people call Neptune."

Dennis and Adir looked at each other. Was
this a joke?

"This is no joke," said the boy, as if he could
read their minds. "I'm on my way." The image
disappeared into the thin mist.

Adir put the rock back into the hole.
"What do we do now?" he asked.

Dennis looked up and pointed. He thought he
saw a flash of bright blue across a cloud.

"I think we should hang around," Dennis said,
watching the sky.

329

ASTRONOMY TODAY

The Fantastic Five

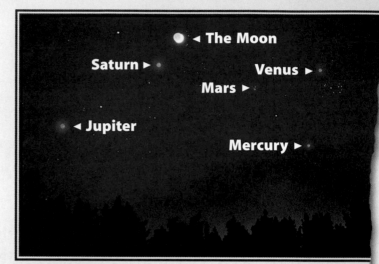

March 27th, 2004

Tonight is a special night for sky watchers. Look up at the sky just after sunset. Five planets will be visible. These are Mercury, Venus, Mars, Saturn, and Jupiter. You do not need a telescope to see them. A simple sky map can tell you where to find the planets. The short show lasts for about an hour after sunset. Then, Mercury drops out of sight.

Right now, the planets are all on the same side of the sun. They are reflecting light from the sun. They look shiny and beautiful. Venus is the brightest planet. You can see all five planets until early April. This unusual event will not happen again until 2036.

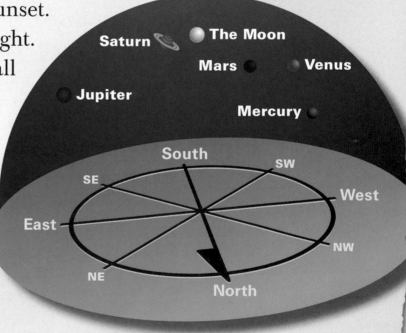

March 27, 2004, 6:30 P.M.

The compass shows how the Fantastic Five line up in relation to the Moon.

Adjectives

Activity One

About Adjectives

Adjectives are words that describe nouns or pronouns. Here are some examples of adjectives: *ten*, *red*, *striped*, *rocky*, *huge*, *colder*, *smallest*. As your teacher reads *The Fantastic Five*, listen carefully for adjectives.

Adjectives in Context

Read *The Fantastic Five* with a partner and make a list of all the adjectives you find. Discuss which noun or pronoun each adjective describes.

Activity Two

Explore Words Together

With a partner, list several adjectives that describe each noun on the right. Compare your list of adjectives with another partner team's.

Earth	space
comet	star
sun	moon

Activity Three

Explore Words in Writing

Write a short descriptive paragraph about the Solar System. Try to use as many adjectives as you can in each sentence. Exchange your paragraphs with a partner. Circle the adjectives in your partner's paragraphs.

The Planets

by Kathleen Ermitage

There are eight official planets in our solar system. These are Mercury, Venus, Earth, Mars, Jupiter, Saturn, Uranus, and Neptune. The planets in our solar system all orbit the sun. They travel in a circular path around the sun. Together, the planets have more than 150 moons.

The inner planets are Mercury, Venus, Earth, and Mars. They are closest to the sun. The inner planets are made mostly of rock.

The outer planets are farthest from the sun. They are Jupiter, Saturn, Uranus, and Neptune. All of the outer planets are balls of gases with rings around them.

What conclusion can you draw about the inner and outer planets?

Sun

Asteroid Belt

Mercury

Venus

Earth

Mars

Mercury

Mercury is the smallest planet and the closest to the sun. It travels around the sun in 88 Earth days. Mercury is rocky. It has craters, valleys, and cliffs.

The temperature on Mercury during the day can be 800 degrees Fahrenheit. On the night side, the temperature is near −300 degrees Fahrenheit.

Fact: Long ago, an asteroid struck Mercury. The state of Texas could fit into the crater left by the asteroid.

Mercury

Venus

Venus is the second planet from the sun. It is the brightest planet in the sky. The thick clouds on Venus reflect sunlight. They also gather heat. The temperature on Venus can reach 900 degrees Fahrenheit.

Why do you think Venus is the brightest planet in our sky?

Fact: Venus spins on its axis very slowly. One day on Venus lasts 243 Earth days!

Venus

Jupiter

Saturn

Uranus

Neptune

Earth

Earth is the third planet from the sun. It takes 365 days to orbit the sun. This is why there are 365 days in a year. Earth has one moon. It orbits Earth in 27 days. Our moon is known as Earth's natural satellite.

Earth's atmosphere is the air for living things to breathe. Seventy percent of the Earth's surface is covered by water. The rest is made up of many different landforms.

Fact: Earth is the only planet with life (as far as we know).

Mars

Mars is the fourth planet from the sun. It is sometimes called the "Red Planet." The mineral iron in the soil makes it red.

Mars has canyons, volcanoes, and ice under its surface. Mars has no sign of water now. Long ago, it may have had rivers and maybe even oceans.

Fact: Mars has two moons. They are the smallest moons in the solar system.

Reverse Think-Aloud Technique Listen as your partner reads part of the text aloud. Choose a point in the text to stop your partner and ask what he or she is thinking about the text at that moment. Then switch roles with your partner.

Earth

What conclusions can you draw about the lack of water on Mars?

Mars

Jupiter

Jupiter is the largest planet. It is the fifth planet from the sun, and it takes about twelve Earth years to orbit the sun. This huge planet is a big ball of storms and gases. They swirl together to make Jupiter's brightly colored clouds. Jupiter has one area called the Great Red Spot. Scientists believe this is a large storm.

Fact: Jupiter is so large that all of the other planets could fit inside of it.

Jupiter

The Great Red Spot

Saturn

Saturn is the second largest planet. It is the sixth planet from the sun. It takes about twenty-nine Earth years to complete one orbit around the sun. Saturn has many bright and beautiful rings. The rings are made of ice and dust.

What can you conclude about a planet's orbit length and its place in the solar system?

Fact: Saturn's largest moon, Titan, is the only moon in our solar system with its own atmosphere and clouds.

Saturn

Uranus

Uranus is the third largest planet and the seventh planet from the sun. Uranus has bright, blue-green clouds. These clouds are caused by a gas called methane. A day on Uranus is equal to 17 Earth hours. This planet has the closest day to Earth's 24 hours.

Fact: Uranus tilts over so far on its axis that it spins on its side.

Uranus

Neptune

Neptune is the fourth largest planet and the farthest from the sun. Neptune takes about 165 Earth years to travel around the sun. It is the only planet that we cannot see directly with our eyes. Neptune's gases make it look like a big, blue ball. Neptune's winds are the strongest in the solar system. They blow more than 1,000 miles per hour on the planet's surface.

Fact: One of Neptune's moons, Triton, is the coldest object measured in space. Triton's surface is −389 degrees Fahrenheit and has ice volcanoes.

Uranus and Neptune are the farthest planets from the sun. What conclusions can you draw about the temperature on these planets?

Neptune

Think and Respond

Reflect and Write

- You and your partner read *The Planets* and told what you were thinking. Discuss your thoughts.

- On one side of an index card, write a conclusion about one of the planets. On the other side, write the text clues and the information you already knew that helped you draw this conclusion.

Adjectives in Context

Search through *The Planets* to find as many adjectives as you can. Write a list of the words you find and share them with a partner. Use these adjectives to write sentences about a new planet you have discovered.

Turn and Talk

INFER: CONCLUSIONS

Discuss with a partner what you have learned so far about how to draw conclusions.

- How can drawing conclusions help you as you read?

Reread page 334 with a partner. Draw at least two conclusions from the text on that page. Share your conclusions and supporting clues with another partner team.

Critical Thinking

With a partner, choose two planets and list what you know about them. Compare the list you made with the information in *The Planets*. Then discuss answers to these questions.

- How do scientists discover new facts about the planets?

- What might make it difficult to learn new information?

PLUTO

WHEN IS A PLANET NOT A PLANET?

In 1930, scientists named Pluto as the ninth planet. In 2006, scientists said Pluto is not a planet. Here's why.

Pluto is smaller than a large **asteroid**. Pluto is mostly rock and ice instead of gas. Unlike planets, Pluto shares its orbit with other objects. It may have once been a **satellite** of Neptune.

In 2003, scientists saw an **image** of something bigger than Pluto. Will this object **appear** as the ninth planet? No **expert** is sure. Stay tuned!

Scientist Clyde Tombaugh discovered Pluto.

Pluto crosses the orbit of Neptune.

Pluto

Neptune

expert   appear   asteroid   image   satellite

Structured Vocabulary Discussion

Work with a partner to complete the following sentences that use the vocabulary words. Discuss your sentences with the class.

It takes an *expert* to . . .

Two objects that *appear* in the night sky are . . .

An *asteroid* is different from a planet because . . .

One kind of *satellite* is . . .

Throughout the week, add to your vocabulary journal entries. Record new insights and other words that relate to this week's vocabulary.

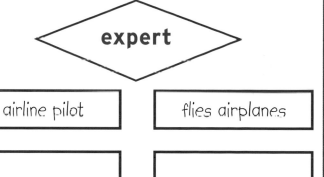

Picture It

Copy this word organizer into your vocabulary journal. In the left column, give examples of someone who is an **expert** at something. In the right column, describe what the person does.

```
          ◇ expert ◇

  ┌──────────────┐   ┌──────────────┐
  │ airline pilot │   │ flies airplanes │
  └──────────────┘   └──────────────┘

  ┌──────────────┐   ┌──────────────┐
  │              │   │              │
  └──────────────┘   └──────────────┘
```

Copy this word chart into your vocabulary journal. Give examples of a favorite **image** you have seen.

image			
a photograph of the Red Sox winning the World Series			

Genre
Photo Essay

KING for a Day

by Austin Woods

Sometimes the moon and Earth form a line with the sun as they orbit. This causes an eclipse. An eclipse occurs when one body in space blocks another. In a solar eclipse, the moon blocks the sunlight. The moon becomes King for a Day!

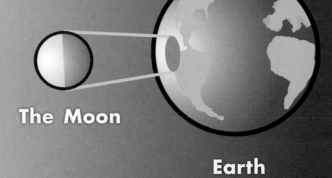

The Moon

Earth

The sky slowly gets dark as the moon moves in front of the sun. The moon's shadow is cast on Earth. This image to the right shows the sun completely blocked by the moon.

Total Solar Eclipse ▶

What Is a Comet?

Comets are a mixture of ice, frozen gases, and dust. They orbit the sun. It would be unusual for you to be able to see comets without a telescope. However, sometimes the unaided eye can see them when they pass close to the sun. The sun's heat melts some of the comet's ice. This leaves a trail of gas and dust. The gas and dust form a comet's tail. The tail reflects sunlight.

The most famous comet is Halley's Comet. Its orbit takes it close to Earth every 76 years. The last fly-by was in 1986. Halley's Comet will remain unseen from Earth until 2061.

Comets may seem unreal, but they are out there. Scientists have counted more than 1000 comets so far. There are more undiscovered comets flying in the sky. Perhaps you will discover the next one!

Halley's Comet

Prefix *un-*

Activity One

About the Prefix *un-*

A prefix is a word part that comes at the beginning of a word. It changes the meaning of the root word. For example, the prefix *un-* means "the opposite of" or "not." Some words with the prefix *un-* are *undo, unknown, unwise, uneven, untidy, unacceptable*. As your teacher reads *What Is a Comet?*, listen for words starting with the prefix *un-*.

The Prefix *un-* in Context

With a partner, read *What Is a Comet?* and make a list of all the *un-* words you find. Discuss how the prefix changes the meaning of each root word.

Activity Two

Explore Words Together

Work with a partner to add the prefix *un-* to each root word on the right. Write a sentence using each new word.

able	fair
happy	certain
kind	clear

Activity Three

Explore Words in Writing

Using words with the prefix *un-*, write sentences about what it might be like to look through a telescope. Exchange your sentences with a partner. Find each word with the prefix *un-* and write new sentences using the word without the prefix.

Sue's Space Rock

by Jin Lee

Sue opened an old toolbox. "Found it!" She held up a large metal block.

"What is it?" asked Mike, her brother.

"It's a magnet!" Sue replied. "A strong one! Grandpa uses it to pick up nails. I'm going to look for meteorites!"

"What? Meteorites are in space," said Mike. "You don't know science," he laughed unkindly.

Sue rolled her eyes. "*Meteors* are rocks that travel in space, but when they fall to Earth they're called *meteorites*. This magnet will help find them. Meteorites have iron in them, so they're magnetic." She taped the magnet to the bottom of a walking stick.

> What details on this page would help you understand the author's purpose for this story?

344

Sue swept the magnet across the ground in the backyard. Mike trailed closely behind.

"It's not going to work," Mike said.

"Then why are you here?" Sue raised her eyebrows. "Let's go to the park," she said. "I bet there are meteorites there."

As they walked to the park, the two took turns sweeping the magnet. The blazing Arizona sun made them uncomfortable. Mike wiped the sweat off his brow. "What does a meteorite even look like?"

"Like a dark rock. It could be really big, too. The largest meteorite found here in Holbrook weighed more than fourteen pounds!"

"People found meteorites here?" Mike asked with surprise.

"In 1912, an enormous meteorite crashed into our town. It broke into thousands of pieces," Sue explained. "Maybe we can find one!"

Why do you think the author wrote a story about meteorites?

Sue and Mike swept their magnet around the park's garden. Suddenly, Sue stopped.

"Wait! I've got something!" A small, dark object was stuck to the bottom of the magnet.

"It's just a bottle cap," she muttered.

"We're never going to find a meteorite," Mike said unhappily. They picked up nails, bolts, and small chunks of metal, but they were unable to pick up a meteorite.

"You told me that meteors fall to Earth. Why don't we find meteorites everywhere?" asked Mike.

"Most of the time, meteors burn up before they hit Earth's surface. That's why you see shooting stars. They're not really stars. They're burning meteors that appear in the night sky," Sue explained.

Say Something Technique Take turns reading a section of text, covering it up, and then saying something about it to your partner. You may say any thought or idea that the text brings to your mind.

How do you think the author wants you to feel about Sue?

346

Sue heard a small thud on her magnet. "We've got something again," she said.

"Probably more junk," said Mike.

Sue carefully lifted a small black rock from the magnet. The rock fit in the palm of her hand, but it was quite heavy.

"It's a meteorite!" beamed Sue.

"Really?" Mike looked unsure.

"See? It looks like a rock, but it's magnetic!"

Mike jumped up and hollered. "Unbelievable! We did it, Sue!"

Sue ran her fingers over the uneven bumps on the cool meteorite. She smiled in wonder. "It is unbelievable. We have a little piece of space now."

Why do you think the author included the details on this page?

347

The next week, a science reporter came to see their meteorite.

"We searched all day," Mike blurted out as soon as the reporter arrived. "Sue never let us give up."

"Let's have a look at what you found," Dr. Jones said. Sue confidently handed over the rock. Dr. Jones pulled out his tools and examined it.

"It's got a thin, shiny black crust. It's cracked a bit, and pale inside," remarked Dr Jones. "And it's got . . ."

". . . rusty spots, from the weathering of nickel and iron," Sue finished.

"That's right," said Dr. Jones with a smile. "Congratulations, it's a meteorite!"

"Awesome," said Mike. "Sue's an expert. I never doubted her! Now if you'll excuse me, I have to look up a word or two in the dictionary!"

Why does the author have a science reporter visit?

Think and Respond

Reflect and Write

- You and your partner have read parts of *Sue's Space Rock* and said something about what you were reading. Discuss your thoughts and ideas.

- On one side of an index card, write a question you had about something the author wrote. On the other side, answer the question and tell how the answer shows the author's purpose.

The Prefix un- in Context

With a partner, search through *Sue's Space Rock* for words with the prefix *un-*. List the words you find. Discuss how the prefix affects the meaning of the root word.

Meteorite

Turn and Talk

ASK QUESTIONS: AUTHOR'S PURPOSE

Discuss with a partner what you have learned so far about how to ask questions about an author's purpose.

- What kind of questions help you find out an author's purpose?

Look at page 345. What clues on this page help you figure out the author's purpose? Share your ideas with a partner.

Critical Thinking

In a small group, brainstorm all that you know about meteors and meteorites. Discuss *Sue's Space Rock* and why meteorites are difficult to find. Then answer these questions.

- Why do you think Sue is looking for a meteorite?

- Do you think you would have a good chance of finding a meteorite? Why or why not?

Contents

Modeled Reading

Shared Reading

Interactive Reading

Floating Home

by David Getz

Appreciative Listening

Appreciative listening means listening for the parts of the story you find funny or amusing. Listen to the focus questions your teacher will read to you.

Man on the Moon

The *Eagle* Has Landed!

July 20, 1969, was an important day. Late that day, a spacecraft called *Eagle* landed on the moon. At around 11:00 P.M. a man climbed out. His name was Neil Armstrong. His **occupation** was **astronaut**. He was the first person to walk on the moon.

The Eagle

One Giant Leap

"That's one small step for a man," Armstrong said, "and one giant leap for mankind." People heard his words across the United States and around the world. Armstrong and another astronaut walked on the moon's surface. They wore special suits to protect against air **pressure** on the moon. They proved that no **challenge** is too **immense** for humanity.

Astronaut on the Moon

Structured Vocabulary Discussion

Read each of the following words or phrases. Then write down the vocabulary word that best matches each one. Discuss with a partner the reasons for your choices.

traveling to the moon   *scientist*

pushing against something   *Neil Armstrong*

outer space

Throughout the week, add to your vocabulary journal entries. Record new insights and other words that relate to this week's vocabulary.

Picture It

Copy this word web into your vocabulary journal. Fill in each circle with a **challenge** you have faced.

learn to play piano

challenge

Copy this word organizer into your vocabulary journal. Name an **occupation** that you would like to have and why you would like to have it.

occupation
athlete, because I love to play sports

Synthesize
Classify/Categorize Information

When you **CLASSIFY** and **CATEGORIZE**, you group things that are the same.

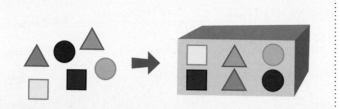

As you read, sort ideas and information into groups.

TURN AND TALK Listen as your teacher reads from *Floating Home* and models how to classify and categorize information. Then with a partner discuss answers to these questions.

- What facts or ideas could be sorted into two different groups?

- What would you call the two groups?

TAKE IT WITH YOU Classifying and categorizing can help you understand how things are alike and different. This will help you bring together information from what you read. As you read other selections, make a chart like the one below to help you classify information into categories.

Categories

Maxine in Earth's atmosphere	Maxine in space

Examples

Weighed 200 pounds Could not move	Weighed nothing at all Was floating

Missions to Mars

by Michelle Sale

Unlike Earth, Mars is a dry, rocky, cold planet. Life is nonexistent there. There are deep valleys, dusty plains, and huge mountains on Mars. One mountain on Mars is the largest in the solar system. It is an inactive volcano. How do we know all this? Scientists use instruments such as flybys, orbiters, and rovers to study Mars.

A *flyby* is a small robotic spacecraft. It flies past a planet and takes hundreds of photographs. Flyby missions gathered the first close pictures of Mars. These pictures showed large craters and the dry, red-looking soil on Mars' surface.

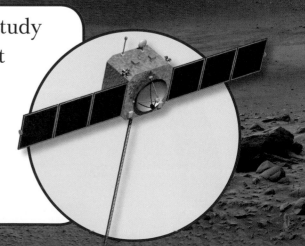

An *orbiter* travels around a planet to study it. One Mars orbiter got caught in a dust storm that lasted a month! Later, it discovered a huge canyon on Mars. The canyon is about 4 times the size of the Grand Canyon in Arizona. The orbiter also found two small moons.

Landers travel on the ground. Most look for signs of life, such as tiny creatures that are invisible to the eye. Landers discovered that the soil on Mars is very dry. Plants cannot grow in Martian soil.

Scientists also use *rovers*. A rover is a remote-controlled car. One rover was delivered to Mars by a parachute. It took pictures and examined rocks. It even kept track of weather on Mars.

In the future, scientists may use special airplanes to explore Mars. They are also building spacecraft to look below the ground for water. Scientists hope to bring rock samples back to Earth. Perhaps a new type of spacecraft will be able to do it!

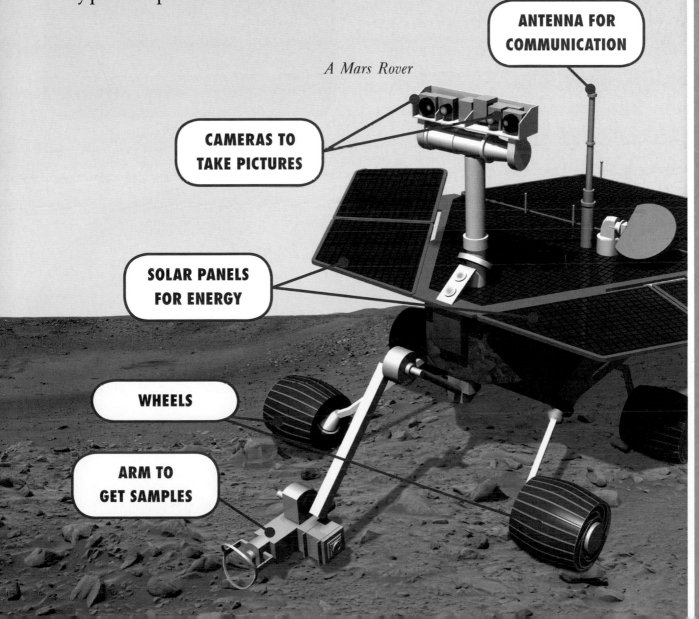

A Mars Rover

ANTENNA FOR COMMUNICATION

CAMERAS TO TAKE PICTURES

SOLAR PANELS FOR ENERGY

WHEELS

ARM TO GET SAMPLES

Space Dogs!

Is it nonsense to think that dogs could rocket into space? Dogs did zoom into space before people did. Scientists used dogs to find out how people would react to space travel. The dogs were helpful.

Belka and *Strelka* were among the first space dogs. Russia sent them into space in 1960. Their spacecraft rocketed from Earth. It was soon invisible. But it didn't disappear. The craft flew around Earth, nonstop, for one day. Then it returned to Earth. The dogs were safe.

Belka and Strelka

Strelka later had puppies. One of Strelka's puppies went to live at the White House with President John F. Kennedy and his family.

The history of space travel would be incomplete without Belka and Strelka, the daring space stogs.

Dog In Space!

Prefixes *non-*, *in-*, and *dis-*

Activity One

About Prefixes *non-*, *in-*, and *dis-*

A *prefix* is a word part that may be added to the beginning of a root word. It changes the root word's meaning. The prefixes *non-*, *in-*, and *dis-* mean "not." The following words have the prefixes *non-*, *in-*, and *dis-*: *nonfiction, nonstop, independent, incomplete, disagree, disbelief*. Listen for words with *non-*, *in-*, and *dis-* as your teacher reads *Space Dogs!*

Prefixes *non-*, *in-*, and *dis-* in Context

With a small group, read *Space Dogs!* Find and list the words with prefixes *non-*, *in-*, and *dis-*. Discuss how the prefix helps you understand the meaning of each word.

Activity Two

Explore Words Together

With a partner, read each root word on the right. Then add the prefix *non-*, *in-*, or *dis-* to make a new word. Discuss what the root word means. Then discuss what the new word with the prefix means.

visible	like
obey	action
sense	stick

Activity Three

Explore Words in Writing

Write sentences to tell whether you think the dogs described in the article were brave and why. Use at least one word with the prefix *non-*, *in-*, or *dis-* in each sentence. Exchange sentences with a partner and circle the *non-*, *in-*, or *dis-* words you find.

Home, Sweet MARS

by Allan Mark

John looked at his computer star map. It showed that Earth and its moon could be seen together in the sky that night. He didn't want to miss such an important event in astronomy.

John stopped at the greenhouse door. "Open," he commanded. The door slid up. John walked past the fruit trees and vegetable plants.

The soil on Mars was filled with harmful chemicals. So John's family and the rest of the colonists grew plants in water melted from polar ice. Dangerous gases filled Mars's atmosphere. So the colonists mixed their own air to breathe indoors.

They had built a huge space station where people worked, shopped, and played.

What important information is there about life on Mars inside and outside the space station?

John sat down near the end of the greenhouse. It was the best place to view the stars and planets. He could see Olympus Mons, the volcano. A storm was forming near it. The winds swirled red dust into the air. John disliked the storms. They sometimes lasted two months.

John touched the computer screen. "Hello, John" the computer said. "What do you need?"

"Hi, Altos," John responded. "Turn on the telescope. Then show Earth and its moon."

While John waited, he began to feel cold air. Since the average temperature on Mars was −67 degrees Fahrenheit, warm air was pumped nonstop through the station's vents.

A chill spread through John's body.

A small cloud of red dust was seeping inside the greenhouse. There was a leak in the glass dome!

How would you classify the information about Mars on this page?

Don't panic! John told himself. "Altos, connect me with Mom. Send the emergency code!"

Immediately, John's mother appeared on the screen. "What's wrong, John?" Captain Lee asked.

"Mom, there's a leak in the greenhouse," answered John.

"I'll call the Health Squad," Captain Lee answered calmly. "Leave the greenhouse through the airlock. It will remove any dust from your clothes and keep dangerous gases out of the space station."

Why would Mars be a dangerous place for people to visit?

John was worried as he entered the airlock. It was dangerous to leave the station. Yet the dome needed to be repaired. There was no way to avoid an outside walk. Captain Lee was trained to work in the Martian environment. But the dust storm made the situation even worse.

John looked through the window and saw that the storm was getting closer. Then he noticed a person climbing the ladder to the roof. Inside the puffy, white suit, he could see his mother taking slow breaths from her air tank. Her air supply would not last long.

John touched his computer. "Altos, show the camera view on top of the greenhouse."

Soon, John could see his mother standing on the glass dome. She took out some tools and began to work on the crack in a panel. The wind swirled dust and rocks. Captain Lee disappeared in a red cloud.

"Hurry up, Mom!" yelled John to himself. "The storm is almost here." John knew that once the storm started, his Mom would be facing wind gusts of up to 375 miles per hour!

What information on this page causes John to worry? How could you categorize this information?

John touched his screen. "Altos, show the entrance view." When the picture appeared, it was incomplete. Dust was blocking the outside cameras. John hoped his mother had gotten inside safely.

What categories would you use to group the scientific information in this story?

"Altos, show the airlock," John said.

A picture of Captain Lee appeared on the screen. John could see his mom standing in the airlock. Oxygen rushed over her spacesuit to remove the dust. John breathed a sigh of relief. She was safe! The crack was repaired.

John looked out the window again. The dust was too thick to see anything. He knew that it would also block the view of Earth.

Disappointed, John wondered if colonists would ever be able to live outside the space station. He hoped so, even if it took a thousand years!

Think and Respond

Reflect and Write

- You and your partner took turns reading and retelling sections of *Home, Sweet Mars*. Discuss your retellings.

- On one side of an index card, write details about life on the Mars colony in the story. On the other side, write categories that you could classify this information into. Discuss your categories with a partner.

Prefixes *non-*, *in-* and *dis-* in Context

Search through *Home, Sweet Mars* for words with the prefixes *non-*, *in-*, and *dis-*. List the words you find. Then write sentences about space travel to Mars using the words from your list.

Turn and Talk

SYNTHESIZE: CLASSIFY/CATEGORIZE INFORMATION

Discuss with a partner what you have learned so far about how to classify and categorize information as you read.

- How can classifying and categorizing information help you understand what you read?

Discuss with a partner how classifying and categorizing information helped you understand *Home, Sweet Mars*.

Critical Thinking

With a partner, discuss what you know about life on Mars. Think about what John's life is like on Mars in *Home, Sweet Mars*. Then answer these questions.

- How is John's life different from your own? Are there any similarities?

- Would you like to explore a planet like Mars? Why or why not?

FOOD THAT FLOATS

Did You Know?

Humans float in space. Astronauts **launch** into space. Once outside of Earth's **atmosphere**, gravity cannot pull people and things down. The astronauts float. Even their food floats! From their spaceship, astronauts can observe Earth, the moon, and the stars. Many astronauts have studied **astronomy** to prepare them for their flight.

Tasty Treats

Space food is made with a special **process**. The food does not need to be stored cold. Space shuttles do not carry refrigerators. Astronauts must **avoid** certain foods, such as salt or crumbly bread. These foods might float inside the spacecraft and damage it. Astronauts eat foods that will not crumble, like tortillas. Their food comes in special packages that won't float away. Astronauts strap meal trays to their laps and enjoy what they can eat!

Structured Vocabulary Discussion

Answer these questions to show you know the meaning of the vocabulary word. Discuss your answers with a partner.

What should you *avoid* on a space flight?

What might you learn from a book on *astronomy*?

What is your *process* of getting ready for school?

> Throughout the week, add to your vocabulary journal entries. Record new insights and other words that relate to this week's vocabulary.

Picture It

Copy this word chart into your vocabulary journal. Fill in the rows with things you could **launch.**

launch
paper airplane

Copy this word web into your vocabulary journal. Fill in the squares with things that might travel through Earth's **atmosphere.**

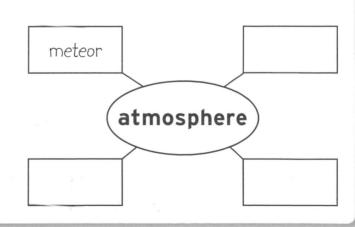

369

Quiet Earth

by Theodore Greenberg

Our time to launch has come and gone,

The rocket's roar now faint,

And our bright Earth below

Shrinks in the night.

True, the globe does glow

With greens, whites, brilliant blues.

Like the sun in the sky,

It seems to glow from the inside.

Even so, it is strange

In this calm and quiet

That "the living planet" Earth

Is what we should call it.

Up here it appears
Much more like a painting—
A sculpture, a snapshot,
Unmoving, unchanging,

So silent and peaceful and quiet—
As if every creature
Might wait, sleeping soundly,
Until our return.

SPACE CAMP

Dear Diary,

Wow! Today was my first day at Space Camp. It was a birthday surprise, prearranged by my parents. For a week, I will learn about space flight.

I want to review every exciting moment of the day. First we toured the U.S. Space and Rocket Center. The place is huge, with buildings spread out over parklands.

Next I sat inside a moving wheel that was like a ride at a fair. I wore a strap to keep me from falling out. The wheel recreated the feeling of being in space.

Space trainers gave us a preview of the week. We will explore a real space capsule. Then we'll plan and pretest a space mission. We'll also live for two days in a space station model. Maybe I'll even revisit the space wheel. I can't wait!

Prefixes *re-* and *pre-*

Activity One

About Prefixes *re-* and *pre-*

A prefix is a word part added to the beginning of a root word. The prefix changes the meaning of the root word. For example, the prefix *re-* means "again". The prefix *pre-* means "before". Examples of words with these prefixes are *retell*, *refill*, *rework*, *preschool*, *preview*, and *prepay*. Listen for words with these prefixes as your teacher reads *Space Camp*.

Prefixes *re-* and *pre-* in Context

Read *Space Camp* and list the words with prefixes *re-* and *pre-*. Make a list for each prefix. Discuss the meaning of each word with a partner.

Activity Two

Explore Words Together

play	write
heat	do
clean	teen

Work with a partner to add *re-* or *pre-* to each word on the right. Some of the words may take either prefix. After you have added prefixes to the words, work together to write the new meaning of each word.

Activity Three

Explore Words in Writing

Write sentences about what you might like to see or do at a space camp. Use as many words as possible that begin with the prefix *re-* or *pre-*. Share your sentences with a partner. Have your partner find each prefix word and tell how the prefix changes the meaning of the root word.

REACH FOR THE STARS!

AMAZING
WOMEN IN SPACE

by Lin Chang

Space travel is filled with firsts. Did you know that the first woman in space was Valentina Tereshkova (Val-en-TEEN-a Tar-es-KOV-a)? She traveled toward the stars in 1963 as a cosmonaut, or Russian astronaut. Read on to review the amazing accomplishments of other women astronauts!

Do you think Valentina Tereshkova was brave to go into space? Why or why not?

1960

1970

1980

1961 Alan Shepard–first American to travel in space

1983 Sally Ride–first American woman to travel in space

1963 Valentina Tereshkova– first woman to travel in space

VALENTINA TERESHKOVA

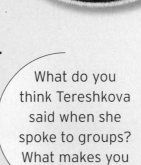

Valentina Tereshkova was born in Russia in 1937. She spent only eight years in school. Then she had to work to make money for her family. She continued to study by mail. She did her lessons at home and sent them back to a school to be graded.

Tereshkova enjoyed parachute jumping. At age 24, she was chosen to train to become a cosmonaut.

In 1963, Tereshkova circled Earth 48 times far above the Earth's atmosphere. She returned in just over two days. Her country named her a hero.

Tereshkova then became an engineer. She also spoke to groups all over the world. Later, she received the United Nations Gold Medal of Peace for her work.

> What do you think Tereshkova said when she spoke to groups? What makes you think so?

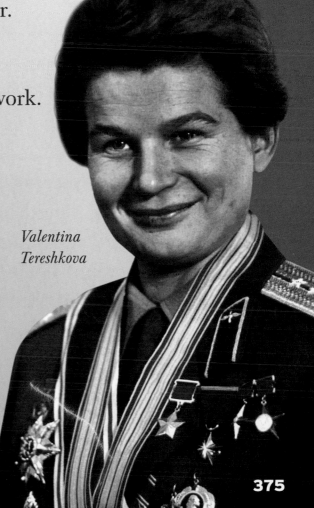

Valentina Tereshkova

1990

2000

1994 Ellen Ochoa–first American Hispanic woman to travel in space

1992 Mae Jemison–first African-American woman to travel in space

375

SALLY RIDE

Sally Ride was born in 1951 in California. She dreamed of becoming a tennis player. In college, she decided to become a scientist. She completed the highest level of study in science.

Then Ride answered a newspaper ad to join the space program. Eight thousand people answered the ad. Only 35 made it through the process for astronaut training. Sally Ride was one of six women accepted in the astronaut program.

In 1983, after a preflight check of the space shuttle, Ride became the first American woman to fly into space. She and the rest of the crew did experiments in space using robots and other special tools.

Later Sally Ride became a college teacher. She retold her space travel stories many times. She even wrote about her work in books for children and adults.

Two-Word Technique Write down two words that reflect your thoughts about each page. Discuss them with your partner.

Why do you think Sally Ride was chosen for the space program? What clues in the passage tell you why?

Sally Ride

MAE JEMISON

Mae Jemison was born in 1956 in Alabama. She was very intelligent. Jemison began college when she was only sixteen years old!

Jemison became a doctor and traveled to Africa after she finished school. She worked in the Peace Corps. Jemison donated her time as a doctor to help people.

> Why do you think the author says Jemison was very intelligent? Give three reasons.

In 1987, Jemison was chosen to be in the space program. In 1992, she became the first African-American woman in space. She did experiments to find out more about plant, animal, and human health in space.

Since leaving the space program, Jemison has started businesses and created programs for schools. She also created a special science camp. Children from all over the world come to this camp to work together to try to resolve world problems.

Mae Jemison

ELLEN OCHOA

Ellen Ochoa was born in 1958 in Los Angeles. She loved playing the flute. She also loved science. She had a decision to make. Should she become a scientist or a flute player? She decided she would do both activities!

Ochoa was still in school when Sally Ride zipped into space. Would it be possible for her to reach for the stars like Sally Ride?

What conclusion can you draw from the fact that Ochoa kept trying to enter the space program?

Ochoa just missed getting into the space program in 1987. She restarted her astronaut training. By 1991, she was a U.S. astronaut. In 1993, she became the first Hispanic woman in space. She was an expert in working with the computers and robots found on spacecrafts.

Ellen Ochoa has an elementary school named after her in her hometown. Like other women astronauts before her, Ellen Ochoa's accomplishments are truly out of this world!

Ellen Ochoa

Think and Respond

Reflect and Write

- You and your partner have read *Reach for the Stars!* and written two words about each page. Discuss your words and thoughts.

- On one side of an index card, write words that describe one of the astronauts. On the other side of the card, write a conclusion you could draw from your description.

Prefixes *re-* and *pre-* in Context

Search through *Reach for the Stars!* for words with the prefixes *re-* and *pre-*. List the words. Then write a short paragraph about space travel using the words.

Turn and Talk

INFER: DRAW CONCLUSIONS

With a partner, discuss what you have learned so far about how to draw conclusions as you read.

- What does it mean to draw conclusions?

- How does drawing conclusions help you in reading?

Look back at *Reach for the Stars!* Discuss with a partner the conclusions you can draw about women astronauts.

Critical Thinking

With a partner, discuss what someone would need to know to become an astronaut. Then answer these questions.

- What did each of the woman astronauts know that helped them to become an astronaut?

- What conclusion can you draw about all of the women astronauts you read about in the selection?

1920's . . . The Migrants Cast Their Ballots, 1974
Jacob Lawrence (1917–2000)

We, the People

Viewing

This painting shows African Americans who moved to Northern cities from the South during the 1920's. At that time, certain laws in the South made it difficult for African Americans to vote. Jacob Lawrence painted many pictures about the "migrants," as he called them.

1. What kind of place is shown in this painting?

2. What do you think the people are reading and talking about as they wait?

3. Why do you think these people are waiting in line to vote? Which person is actually voting? How can you tell?

4. What do you think the people at the table are doing? Why?

In This UNIT

In this unit, you will read about how laws are made. You will also read about why voting and electing leaders is important.

Making Laws

Contents

Modeled Reading

Shared Reading

Interactive Reading

CHickens May Not Cross the Road and Other Crazy (But True) Laws

Kathi Linz

Illustrated by **Tony Griego**

Precise Listening

Precise listening means listening for details. Listen to the focus questions your teacher will read to you.

The Great Debate at Kennedy Elementary

"Welcome to the final **debate** for mayor!" said Principal Law. "Our students will ask the candidates questions today."

"I have a question for Mr. Cruz," said Penny. "I would like to ride a horse to school. Can you make that **legal**?"

"The town **officials** do not plan to debate about **granting** permission for students to ride animals to school," said Mr. Cruz. "However, you are welcome to ride the bus!"

"The next question is from Bill," said the principal.

"What's your stand on Pizza Fridays, Mayor Kim?" asked Bill. "Do you want to take away pizza!"

"No, I don't, Bill," said Mayor Kim. "But, I would like to add a salad to Friday's menu. I believe in **representation** from all the food groups!"

Structured Vocabulary Discussion

With a partner, finish each sentence to show what the vocabulary word means. Discuss your choices with the class.

- At home, the *debate* was about *granting* me . . .

- People who are *officials* must . . .

- Having *representation* is an important part of government because . . .

- Knowing what is *legal* is important because . . .

Throughout the week, add to your vocabulary journal entries. Record new insights and other words that relate to this week's vocabulary.

Picture It

Copy this word wheel into your vocabulary journal. Name a topic you would like to discuss in a **debate**.

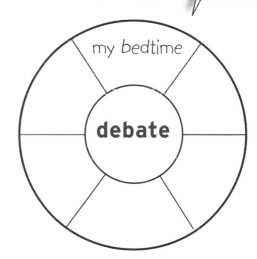

my bedtime

debate

Copy this word chart into your vocabulary journal. Fill in the first column with things that are **legal**. Fill in the second column with related things that are not **legal**.

legal	not legal
riding a bike	driving a car without a license

Monitor Understanding
Strategic Reading

STRATEGIES help you understand what you read.

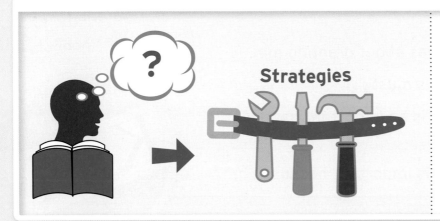

When you don't understand, think about the strategies you know and try them.

TURN AND TALK Listen as your teacher reads from *Chickens May Not Cross the Road* and models how to do strategic reading. Then discuss answers to these questions.

• Did you find any part of the text difficult to understand?

• What strategy can you use to better understand the text?

TAKE IT WITH YOU Using reading strategies can help you understand difficult parts of a text. As you read other selections, try to choose the best reading strategy to help you when you have trouble understanding meaning. Use a chart like the one below to help you do strategic reading.

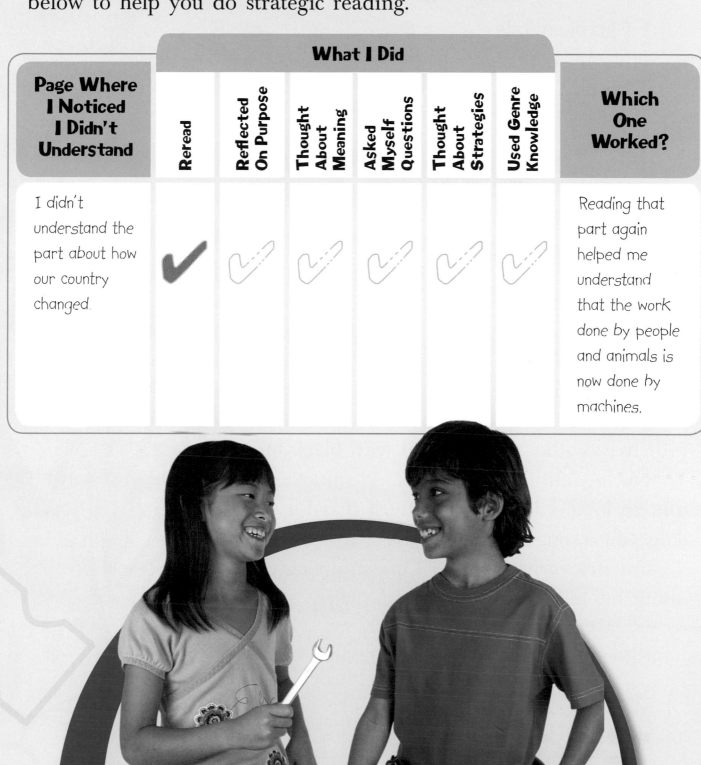

Page Where I Noticed I Didn't Understand	What I Did						Which One Worked?
	Reread	Reflected On Purpose	Thought About Meaning	Asked Myself Questions	Thought About Strategies	Used Genre Knowledge	
I didn't understand the part about how our country changed.	✓	✓	✓	✓	✓	✓	Reading that part again helped me understand that the work done by people and animals is now done by machines.

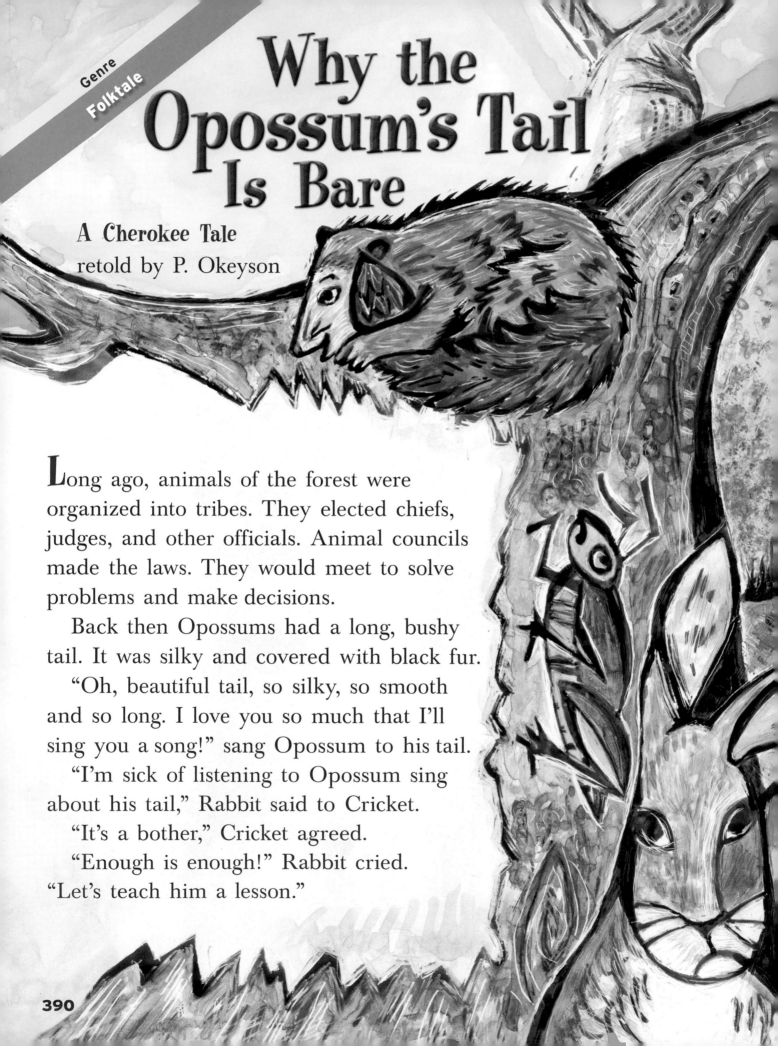

Why the Opossum's Tail Is Bare

A Cherokee Tale
retold by P. Okeyson

Long ago, animals of the forest were organized into tribes. They elected chiefs, judges, and other officials. Animal councils made the laws. They would meet to solve problems and make decisions.

Back then Opossums had a long, bushy tail. It was silky and covered with black fur.

"Oh, beautiful tail, so silky, so smooth and so long. I love you so much that I'll sing you a song!" sang Opossum to his tail.

"I'm sick of listening to Opossum sing about his tail," Rabbit said to Cricket.

"It's a bother," Cricket agreed.

"Enough is enough!" Rabbit cried. "Let's teach him a lesson."

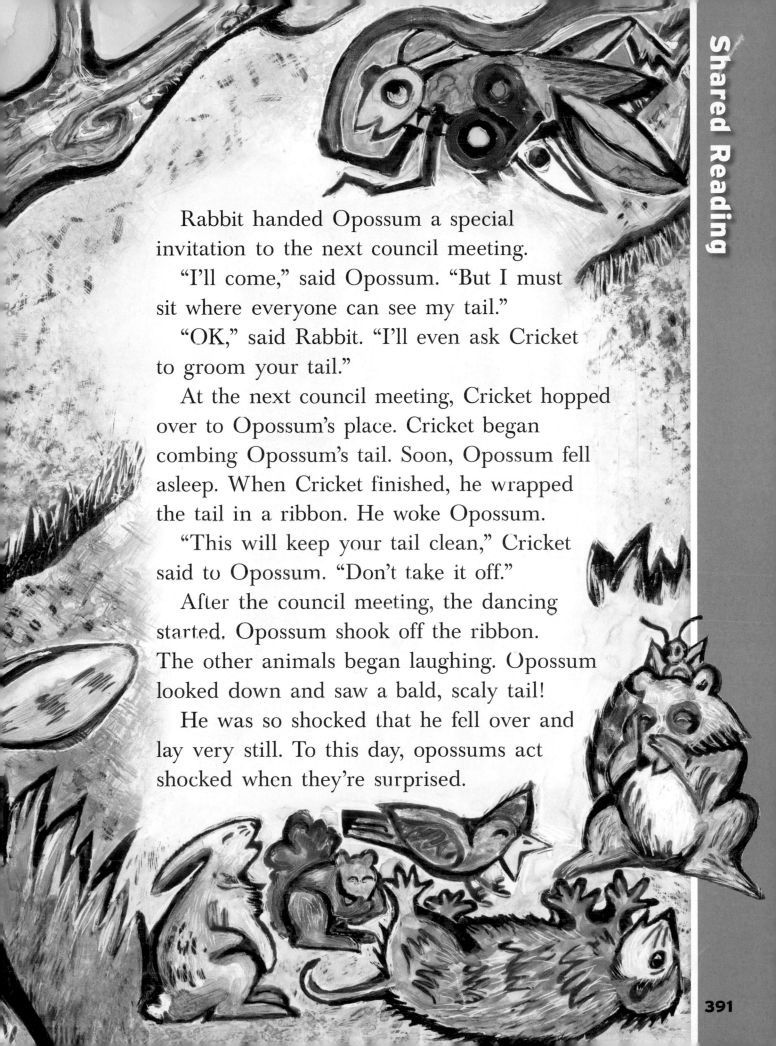

Rabbit handed Opossum a special invitation to the next council meeting.

"I'll come," said Opossum. "But I must sit where everyone can see my tail."

"OK," said Rabbit. "I'll even ask Cricket to groom your tail."

At the next council meeting, Cricket hopped over to Opossum's place. Cricket began combing Opossum's tail. Soon, Opossum fell asleep. When Cricket finished, he wrapped the tail in a ribbon. He woke Opossum.

"This will keep your tail clean," Cricket said to Opossum. "Don't take it off."

After the council meeting, the dancing started. Opossum shook off the ribbon. The other animals began laughing. Opossum looked down and saw a bald, scaly tail!

He was so shocked that he fell over and lay very still. To this day, opossums act shocked when they're surprised.

Minnesota's State Muffin

All states have symbols, such as a state bird or a state song. State laws decide these symbols. Some states have state foods. In Minnesota they even have a state muffin. It's the blueberry muffin. This became a law because of a third grade class.

Third graders in Carlton, Minnesota were studying how bills become laws. They decided to make their own law. The students knew their state had symbols. But it didn't have a state muffin. Why couldn't it be the blueberry muffin?

The class asked a lawmaker to support a muffin bill. The bill was introduced to the state government. When the lawmakers voted, the bill passed. The governor signed it into law.

Maybe you aren't old enough to vote. But it doesn't mean you can't help make laws!

Contractions

Minnesota

Activity One

About Contractions

A contraction is a shortened form of two words that are put together. An apostrophe takes the place of the missing letter or letters. For example, *I'm* is a contraction for *I am*. Here are some other contractions: *we've = we have*, *shouldn't = should not*, *what's = what is*. As your teacher reads *Minnesota's State Muffin*, listen for the contractions.

Contractions in Context

Read *Minnesota's State Muffin* with a partner. Write a list of the contractions you find. Next to each contraction, write the two words that make up each contraction.

Activity Two

Explore Words Together

Work with a partner to make each pair of words on the right into a contraction. List the contractions you made and be ready to share them with the rest of the class.

you have	let us
is not	she is
I will	they are

Activity Three

Explore Words in Writing

Write three silly laws. Use at least one contraction in each law. Then read your laws aloud to a partner. Have your partner identify each contraction.

Councilman Haass Makes a Difference

by Michelle Budzilowicz

Who makes the laws in your town or city? Chip Haass is a city councilman from San Antonio, Texas. He represents District 10. A district is an area of a city. It's like a big neighborhood. Each district elects a representative to the City Council. Councilmen and councilwomen govern the city.

Councilman Haass has lived in San Antonio all his life. When he's not working for the city, he likes to play golf. He also likes to watch baseball. When he was in 3rd grade, Haass wanted to be a professional baseball player. But the people of San Antonio are happy that he is now a city councilman.

Read on to find out what Councilman Haass' job is all about.

How could rereading or reading more slowly help you better understand this page?

Councilman Chip Haass

San Antonio Skyline

How long have you been a member of the City Council?

I have been elected twice. Each term is two years long. That's a total of four years. I started my first term in June, 2003. Then I was reelected two years later. I cannot run for reelection in 2007.

Why did you decide to run for City Council?

Friends and people in my community thought I would be a good representative. I could help make and pass laws that would make a difference. My favorite part of my job is helping people.

Voice Recorder Used for Interviews

How did you run your campaign?

I didn't have a lot of money to pay for my campaign. My friends and supporters helped me. We worked very hard. Everyday we talked to people. We walked block to block. We knocked on voters' doors. It was tiring, but also very rewarding.

What strategy helped you understand what the councilman's campaign was like?

The San Antonio City Council, 2005–2007

How did you get elected for City Council?

The people in my district elected me. I had the most votes in my district. So I won!

Read, Cover, Remember, Retell Technique With a partner, take turns reading as much text as you can cover with your hand. Then cover up what you read and retell the information to your partner.

How did you feel when you were elected?

I was very excited and happy. The hard work had paid off. I was ready to start my new job. Mostly I was excited to help my community. The people in my district elected me to serve them.

The Alamo in San Antonio

Where did you give your acceptance speech?

Because I was elected twice, I got to give two speeches. In 2003, I gave a speech to family

What questions do you have about this page? How does asking questions help you understand the text better?

and friends at a private home. In 2005, I had a big Election Watch party. There were about three hundred people there!

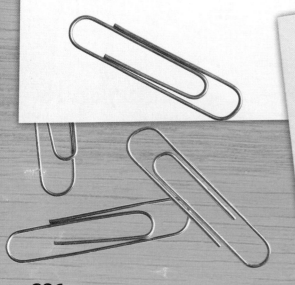

City Government

- Mayor
- City Council
- Municipal Court

What do you do in a typical day?

My staff and I try to solve problems for people in our district. For example, we try to get sidewalks fixed. We try to have trash picked up from places where it's been left. I have meetings with different groups. Then I meet with different city departments. On Thursdays we have City Council Session. We talk about how to solve the city's larger problems. It's a long meeting. It goes from 9:00 A.M. until 6:00 P.M.

What is the most important issue you've worked on?

I try to improve the community any way I can. I have worked to improve the roads in my district. This includes fixing potholes and bumps. I have worked on making the parks better. I've also worked on keeping the city's environment clean.

The City Council meets at San Antonio City Hall.

What strategy did you use on this page to understand what you read?

What bills are you working on now?

I'm working on getting a Hike and Bike trail. It will be free of cars. It will connect city parks. This will give people a chance to enjoy the parks. I think it's important for people to get outside and enjoy where they live!

What reading strategy would help you understand the information on this page?

What makes your job interesting?

I like helping people. There are always new issues to deal with. Each day there's something new to do to help people.

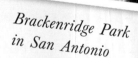

Brackenridge Park in San Antonio

Since third graders can't vote, how can they make a difference in politics?

Third graders can make a difference by talking to their parents and friends about safety in their streets and neighborhoods. Third graders can also help by working hard in school. Reading and writing are very important. Someday you may be reading and writing new laws for your City Council!

The River Walk in San Antonio

398

Think and Respond

Reflect and Write

- You and your partner took turns reading and retelling sections of *Councilman Haass Makes a Difference*. Discuss what you and your partner said to one another.

- On one side of an index card, describe a part of the text that was difficult to understand. On the other side, write what strategy you used to make the meaning more clear.

Contractions in Context

Search through *Councilman Haass Makes a Difference* and list the contractions you find. Write the two words each contraction comes from. Then circle the letter or letters that were left out to make the contraction.

Turn and Talk

MONITOR UNDERSTANDING: STRATEGIC READING

Discuss with a partner what you have learned so far about how to use strategic reading.

- Why do you use reading strategies to monitor your understanding?

With a partner, look back at page 395. Write what reading strategies you used on this page. Compare your reading strategies to another partner team's.

TEXAS

San Antonio ★

Critical Thinking

Return to *Councilman Haass Makes a Difference*. In a small group, list what Councilman Haass does for his community. Then list things that you think your town or city council should work on in your community. Then discuss answers to these questions.

- Why do you think city councils are important?

- How could you help your town or city council to make your community a better place?

THE FIRST WOMAN MAYOR

Susanna Salter was the first woman elected to the office of mayor. Voters in Argonia, Kansas, elected her in 1887.

Salter did not plan to be a **candidate**. Her name was put on the ballot as a joke. The people who did this thought that few people would vote for a woman.

▲ *Susanna Salter was 27 when she was elected mayor.*

An Election Day Surprise

In 1887, women in Argonia had won the right to vote for mayor. They helped elect Salter. Some men voted for her, too.

Many people felt that **justice** had been done. Instead of being a joke, Salter had the **authority** to **govern**. She served her term well. But she did not stay in **politics**.

▼ *In 1887, women in Kansas were allowed to vote only in some local elections.*

Structured Vocabulary Discussion

When your teacher says a vocabulary word, your small group will take turns saying the first word that comes to mind. When your teacher says "Stop," the last person to say a word should explain how that word is related to the vocabulary word.

Throughout the week, add to your vocabulary journal entries. Record new insights and other words that relate to this week's vocabulary.

Picture It

Copy this word chart into your vocabulary journal. Write reasons why someone would and would not be a good **candidate** for an office like class president.

good candidate	not a good candidate
works hard	

Copy this word web into your vocabulary journal. Fill in the circles with examples of people who have **authority**.

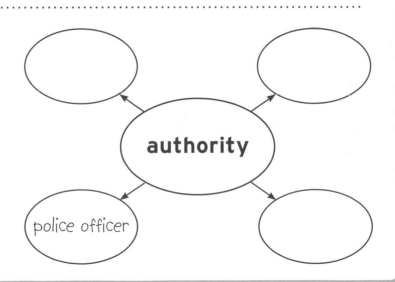

401

If My Mom Made the Laws

by Sarah Hughes

You should hear what my mom says.
She's always making laws.
Luckily for you and me,
You can't make laws "just because."

"There ought to be a law," she says,
"For how much TV you watch a day.
That goes the same for video games,
And how many hours you can play."

"There ought to be a law," she says,
"For how high you can swing in the park,
Or how long you can hang upside down,
Or keep the lights on after dark."

"There ought to be a law," she says,
"For how often you hug your mother,
And how much fruit you eat a day,
And how long you read to your brother."

"There ought to be a law," she says,
"That makes sure you're nice and polite,
That you have to say *please* and *thank you*,
And that your mother is always right!"

"There ought to be a law," she says,
But she does not have the authority
To make the laws for anyone—
Except my brother and me!

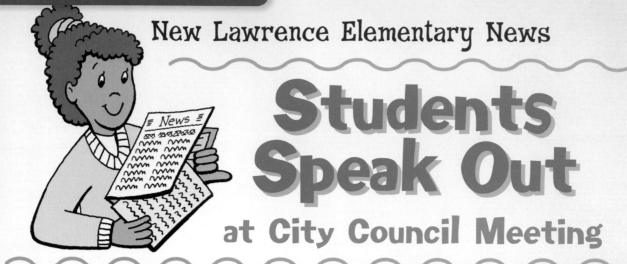

New Lawrence Elementary News

Students Speak Out
at City Council Meeting

New Lawrence, CT—Last night, new voices were heard at the City Council meeting. Students came to exercise their rights. They came to ask for a traffic light. And they came prepared.

The students brought a petition, or request, for a light at Waldorf St. and Avenue D. It was signed by more than five hundred townspeople.

One student pointed out how drivers had trouble seeing at the intersection.

"I'm afraid one of them might not see my brother and me when we cross," she said.

"I can see you put a lot of work into this petition," said District 12 councilman Matt Broder. He said the city council would vote on it.

"I'm glad they listened to us," said one student. "We've proved that our idea was a good one."

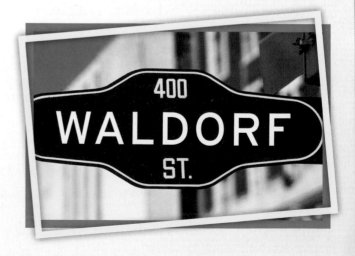

Pronouns

Activity One

About Pronouns

A noun is a word that names a person, place, or thing. A pronoun takes the place of a noun. For example, the pronoun *she* or *he* can take the place of the noun *student*:

The *student* ran for class president.

She wanted to make changes at school.

Other pronouns include *I, we, they, them, you, her, mine* and *our.* As your teacher reads *Students Speak Out at City Council Meeting*, listen for the pronouns.

Pronouns in Context

Read *Students Speak Out at City Council Meeting*. Write a list of all the pronouns you can find. Next to each pronoun write the noun it stands for.

Activity Two

Explore Words Together

Work with a partner to think of pronouns that could replace the nouns shown on the right. List your pronouns and be ready to share them with the class.

Maria	monkeys
team	Billy
desk	flowers

Activity Three

Explore Words in Writing

Write several sentences describing what you think a city council meeting might be like. Use several nouns (names and things) and pronouns in your sentences.

Town Watch

by Juana Salazar

The salty sea air bit Hans' nose. His voyage from Germany to the United States had been a long one. Hans grabbed his bag and walked slowly behind his parents off the ship. His two younger sisters followed close behind him. He knew many days of travel still lay ahead.

"Philadelphia!" his dad cried. "It means *city of brotherly love.* We will make our new home there."

Wagons carried Hans and his family from New York to Philadelphia. The year was 1700. Dust swirled in the air. It stung Hans' eyes and got into his nose and mouth. Just when he thought he couldn't stand another day of travel, Hans saw the town of Philadelphia up ahead. A wide grin crossed his face.

What important information do you learn on this page?

Philadelphia was a busy place. Horse buggies and wagons clomped in every direction. People carried bundles of different sizes. Hans wondered what was inside them. He wondered about many things, but he was too shy to ask questions. He thought that if he stood quietly and watched, many of his questions would be answered.

What kind of questions do you think Hans has about his new home?

Hans and his family quickly found their new home. It was near the busy center of town. Hans didn't mind that the house was small. He knew that many new opportunities lay ahead.

The next night Hans' father met with many of their new neighbors. Hans watched the candle flame flicker near his bed as he drifted off to sleep. He wondered what stories his father would have to share.

In the morning, Hans' father looked troubled.

"I can't believe it!" his father said. "The city is not safe. It is not a city of brotherly love after the sun goes down. Criminals roam the dark streets. They do harm to honest folk. There does not seem to be any justice. This is no way to live."

Hans worried. "Have we made a mistake?" he asked his parents.

Hans' mom smiled. "We will make it work," she said. "We will join the honest folk here, and we will do all we can."

In town later that day, Hans wanted to ask other children what they could do to help the town, but he was too shy. He couldn't force the words to come out. He still was worried about his family.

Say Something Technique Take turns reading a section of text, covering it up, and then saying something about it to your partner. You may say any thought or idea that the text brings to your mind.

How would you classify the information Hans' father tells Hans?

At town meetings, Hans' father and many others talked about how to make Philadelphia safer. They all came up with an idea to establish a "safe streets" plan. A person with a bell would be on watch and ring it when there was danger. Then others would come help.

How is the "safe streets" plan similar to and different from the way your neighborhood is protected?

Hans went with his father to the next town meeting. They rushed to get to the meeting on time. Hans' father tripped on an old horseshoe in the road. "Get the town doctor for me!" he cried.

Hans raced to get the doctor. The doctor took Hans' dad to his office. "I will have to stitch this wound," the doctor said. "Come back for your father in an hour."

"But the meeting—" Hans said. "My father has new ideas."

Hans' dad looked him in the eye. "You will have to tell them," he said. "Now, go quickly!"

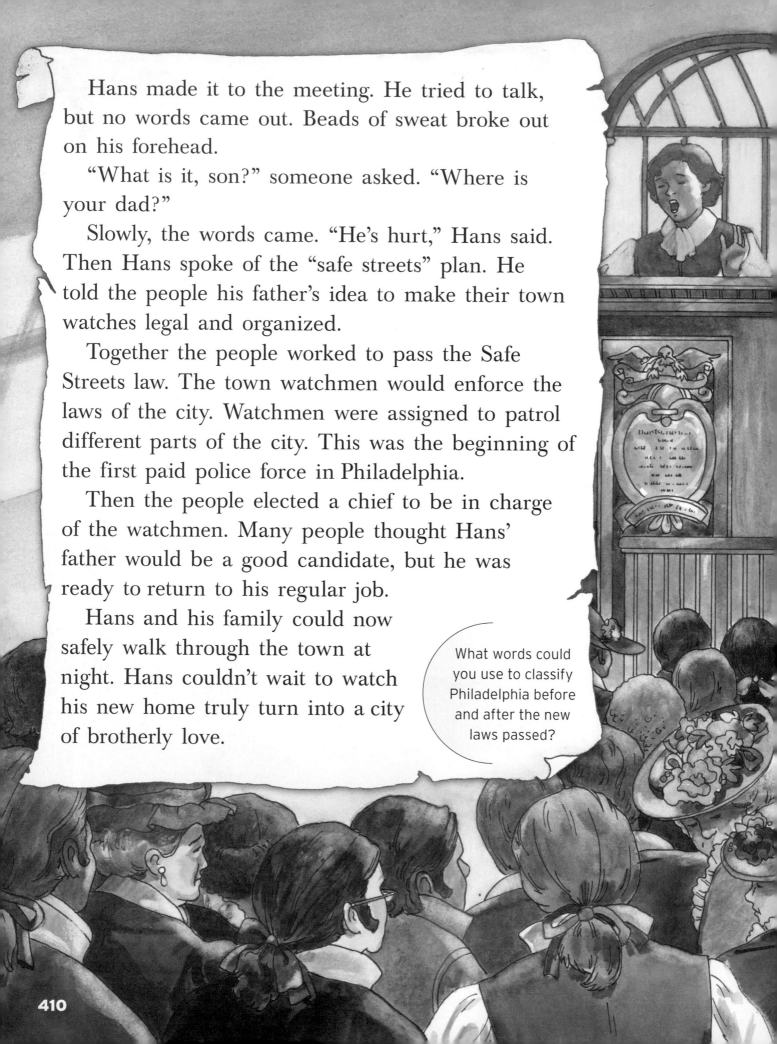

Hans made it to the meeting. He tried to talk, but no words came out. Beads of sweat broke out on his forehead.

"What is it, son?" someone asked. "Where is your dad?"

Slowly, the words came. "He's hurt," Hans said. Then Hans spoke of the "safe streets" plan. He told the people his father's idea to make their town watches legal and organized.

Together the people worked to pass the Safe Streets law. The town watchmen would enforce the laws of the city. Watchmen were assigned to patrol different parts of the city. This was the beginning of the first paid police force in Philadelphia.

Then the people elected a chief to be in charge of the watchmen. Many people thought Hans' father would be a good candidate, but he was ready to return to his regular job.

Hans and his family could now safely walk through the town at night. Hans couldn't wait to watch his new home truly turn into a city of brotherly love.

What words could you use to classify Philadelphia before and after the new laws passed?

410

Think and Respond

Reflect and Write

- You and your partner read *Town Watch* and said something about the part you read. Discuss your thoughts and ideas.

- On one side of an index card, classify the problems that Hans faces in Philadelphia. Put the problems into categories. On the other side, explain how the problems were solved.

Pronouns in Context

Search through *Town Watch* for pronouns. List the pronouns you find, and share them with a partner. Then write the noun each pronoun replaced.

Turn and Talk

SYNTHESIZE: CLASSIFY/CATEGORIZE INFORMATION

Discuss with a partner what you have learned about how to classify or categorize information.

- How can classifying or categorizing information help you understand what you read?

Discuss with a partner important information in the story. Then classify this information into categories.

Critical Thinking

In a small group, discuss how the people in Philadelphia in 1700 made their streets safe. Brainstorm things that would make your community a safer place. Then discuss answers to these questions.

- What did you learn in *Town Watch* about how people can make their community a safe place?

- What would you do if you wanted to make a new law?

Contents

Every Vote Counts

Modeled Reading

Shared Reading

Interactive Reading

DUCK

FOR
PRESIDENT

BY DOREEN CRONIN

ILLUSTRATED BY BETSY LEWIN

Strategic Listening

Strategic listening means listening to make sure you understand the story. Listen to the focus questions your teacher will read to you.

HELP WANTED!
President of the United States

Do you love your country? Do you want to do your **civic** duty? Maybe you will be the president of the United States! You would sign bills into law and choose judges. You would travel all over the world and meet with world leaders.

To apply for this job, you must be an American citizen born in this country. You must be at least 35 years old. You must be willing to move to Washington, DC. The job lasts four years (with the possibility of four more). The people of the United States **encourage** all qualified people to apply!

You must be comfortable giving a **speech** in front of a **crowd**.

You must be willing to accept criticism. Sometimes people will **protest** your decisions.

Structured Vocabulary Discussion

Work with a partner to complete the following sentences about the vocabulary words.

Encourage and *protest* are different because . . .

Speech and *crowd* are related because . . .

Voting is a *civic* duty because . . .

Throughout the week, add to your vocabulary journal entries. Record new insights and other words that relate to this week's vocabulary.

Picture It

Copy this word wheel into your vocabulary journal. Fill in the sections of the circle with jobs that require people to make a **speech**.

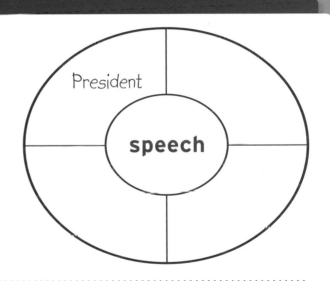

President

speech

Copy this word organizer into your vocabulary journal. In the top box, describe a **crowd**. In the bottom box, give an example of where you might see a crowd.

crowd

close together

at a game

The White House

417

Comprehension Strategy

Create Images
Revise

CHANGE your MENTAL IMAGE as you read.

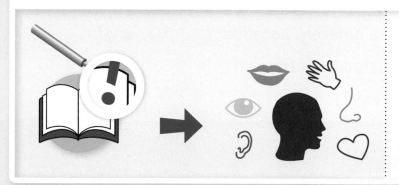

As you read, think about how the mental images in your mind change as the text gives you new information.

TURN AND TALK Listen as your teacher reads from *Duck for President* and models how to create mental images and revise them. Then discuss with a partner the answers to these questions.

- How did you picture Duck in your mind at the very beginning of the story?

- How did your image of Duck change? What parts of the text changed your image of Duck?

TAKE IT WITH YOU Creating and revising images in your mind as you read makes you a better reader. As you read other selections, create and revise images in your mind. This new information will help you better understand what you read.

In the Text	Image for this Section	How Did My Image Change?
I read to the page where Duck is doing chores on a farm and getting dirty.	My mental image is of a duck with grass and bits of mud stuck to its body.	
I read to the page where Duck decides to run for governor.	My mental image is of Duck in a suit. He is on the campaign trail, so he goes out to meet people. He is funny because he is still a duck!	My image changed from thinking of Duck as an animal to thinking of him as a person. He is funny.

HISTORY'S WITNESS

by Molly Smith

I was a freshman in college when I first voted. I had just turned eighteen. It was 1992, a presidential election year.

Election Day came closer. I suddenly realized I was registered to vote in Massachusetts. But I was away at school in Washington, D.C. I couldn't go home to vote.

My mother told me about absentee ballots. An absentee ballot would allow me to vote by mailing a ballot to my hometown. My mother requested an absentee ballot from the town clerk. The clerk quickly sent it to me.

The election was three weeks away. But I filled out my ballot immediately! First I checked the box for the presidential candidate. Then I voted for local elections and issues. Last, I proudly mailed my ballot in.

Bill Clinton was elected president of the United States of America in 1992. Thousands of people gathered for his inauguration.

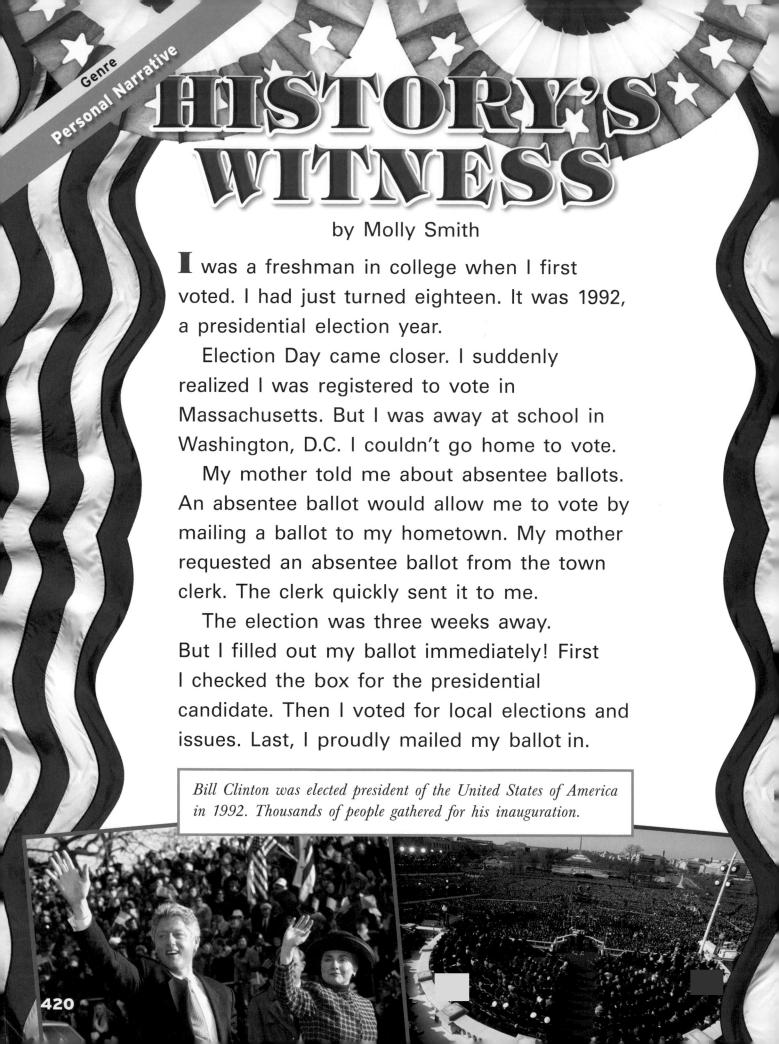

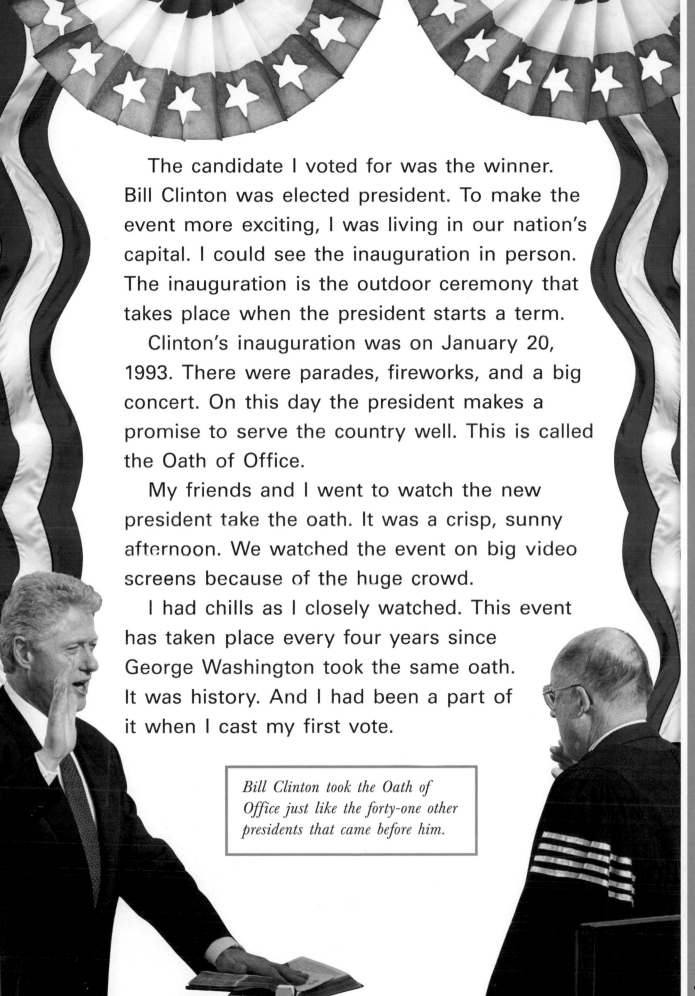

The candidate I voted for was the winner. Bill Clinton was elected president. To make the event more exciting, I was living in our nation's capital. I could see the inauguration in person. The inauguration is the outdoor ceremony that takes place when the president starts a term.

Clinton's inauguration was on January 20, 1993. There were parades, fireworks, and a big concert. On this day the president makes a promise to serve the country well. This is called the Oath of Office.

My friends and I went to watch the new president take the oath. It was a crisp, sunny afternoon. We watched the event on big video screens because of the huge crowd.

I had chills as I closely watched. This event has taken place every four years since George Washington took the same oath. It was history. And I had been a part of it when I cast my first vote.

> *Bill Clinton took the Oath of Office just like the forty-one other presidents that came before him.*

VOTE... NOW!

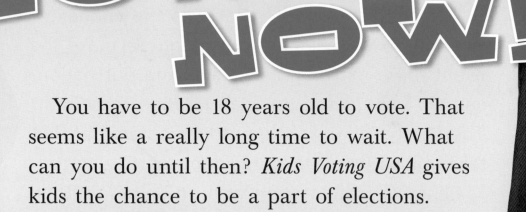

You have to be 18 years old to vote. That seems like a really long time to wait. What can you do until then? *Kids Voting USA* gives kids the chance to be a part of elections.

Kids usually join the program in school. Students register to vote with *Kids Voting USA* in class. They learn about candidates and the issues. This helps kids vote more wisely. They are well prepared for Election Day when they fill out a *Kids Voting USA* ballot.

The ballot looks exactly like a real ballot. The votes are counted across the country. The results are always posted online after the regular election. In some places, the voting results are even on TV!

More than a million kids voted through this program in the last presidential election. *Kids Voting USA* strongly believes these same kids will vote in the future—for real!

Voters Register Here!

Adverbs

Activity One

About Adverbs

An adverb is a word that describes a verb, another adverb, or an adjective. Adverbs answer such questions as *how? when?* and *where?* For example: *The politician spoke loudly.* In this sentence, *loudly* is an adverb. It describes how the politician spoke. Other examples of adverbs are: *quickly, slowly, badly, often, never, outside, here,* and *there.* Listen for adverbs as your teacher reads *Vote . . . Now!*

Adverbs in Context

Look back through *Vote . . . Now!* Find each adverb. Then identify the word or phrase that each adverb describes. Make a list of all the adverbs.

Activity Two

Explore Words Together

With a partner, take turns making up a sentence using each of the verbs on the right. In each sentence, use an adverb that describes the verb.

voted	walking
ran	listen
feel	learn

Activity Three

Explore Words in Writing

Write two sentences about the president of the United States without using an adverb. Exchange sentences with a partner. Add adverbs to your partner's sentences, and then have your partner circle the adverbs.

Genre
Realistic Fiction

On the Campaign Trail

by Lewis Hoff

Luis and his mother stepped out of the car. Immediately, a crowd of reporters rushed over. Click! Flash! Luis smiled as the reporters snapped pictures. He had eaten a hot dog at lunch and hoped there wasn't any mustard on his face.

"Mrs. Sanchez, will you vote for a tax increase to pay for education?" one reporter asked.

Mrs. Sanchez responded cheerfully as she guided Luis into her campaign headquarters.

"Your dad will pick you up," she told Luis. "I've got another meeting, so I'll be home late."

Luis was really proud of his mother. She had served on the school board, but now she was running for election to the Texas House of Representatives. Luis knew that his mother would do a great job, but he was tired of meetings, crowds, and most of all, the reporters.

"Four more days," Luis told himself.

What was the first image that came to your mind as you began reading?

424

The next day was Saturday. Many volunteers gathered at the Sanchez house. They were planning to pass out flyers in the neighborhood.

"This race is very close," announced Mrs. Sanchez. "We have to let the voters know what I will do if I'm elected."

Luis and his mother must have knocked on one hundred doors in three hours. Along the way, Mrs. Sanchez shook hands with the people she met. She spoke with several reporters, too. Luis waited patiently in the hot sun as his mother talked. He wiped the sweat off his face using his shirtsleeve. Click! Flash! Luis groaned, hoping that picture wouldn't appear in the newspaper!

Only three more days now, sighed Luis.

What information on this page helped you form a new picture in your mind?

DAILY PL

On Sunday, Mrs. Sanchez gave a speech at a community picnic. Luis was always proud when his mother talked about her Hispanic heritage. She told the story of her parents. They had come to the United States from Mexico and had become U. S. citizens. After the speech, everyone clapped and cheered loudly. Once again, the reporters were everywhere. Click! Flash! One reporter snapped a picture as Luis yawned.

"Another two days!" thought Luis.

On Monday, Mrs. Sanchez was already on the phone when Luis left for school. He peeked over his mother's shoulder and looked at her calendar. Mrs. Sanchez had two meetings, a press conference, and two speeches.

"Tomorrow is the deadline," thought Luis. *"One more day!"*

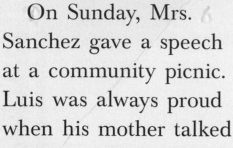

At last, it was Tuesday. Mrs. Sanchez drove Luis to school. His school was a polling site, a place where people vote. Mrs. Sanchez wanted to talk to people as they came to the polls to vote. Already people were standing by the road waving signs for different candidates. He saw lots of blue and white signs with his mother's name.

"Good luck, Mom!" Luis said.

Throughout the day, Luis watched people come and go from the school. He hoped they were voting for his mother. When the school bell finally rang, Mr. Sanchez picked Luis up. They drove to a hotel to wait for the election results.

> What mental image do you have of Luis on election day? What details help you create the image?

"How is the race going for Mom?" Luis asked.

"It's too early to tell," Mr. Sanchez answered. "We have to wait until the polls close."

Many supporters and reporters were gathering at the hotel to hear the outcome of the election. So far, Mrs. Sanchez was in the lead.

Click! Flash! One reporter snapped a picture of Luis as he wiped cookie crumbs off his shirt. He hoped that was the last picture.

Just before midnight, Mrs. Sanchez received a phone call from the other candidate. After a moment, a huge smile spread across her face.

She climbed the stairs to the stage. Luis quickly followed his mother.

Mrs. Sanchez spoke excitedly. "Dear friends, I am pleased to announce that I am the newest Texas representative."

A huge cheer filled the room. Luis happily hugged his mother. Click! Flash! It was one picture that Luis didn't mind.

How has your mental image of an election changed after reading this story?

VOTE
Sanchez

Think and Respond

Reflect and Write

- You and your partner have read *On the Campaign Trail* and asked each other questions. Discuss those questions and your answers.

- With your partner, write one of your images from early in the story on one side of an index card. On the other side, write how that image changed as you read the story.

Adverbs in Context

Search through *On the Campaign Trail* to find adverbs. Make a list of your words and compare your list with a partner's.

Turn and Talk

CREATE IMAGES: REVISE

Discuss with a partner what you have learned so far about creating and revising images.

- How do you use details to create and revise images as you read?

With a partner, discuss how you pictured a political campaign before you read the story. Discuss how your image of a campaign changed after you read *On the Campaign Trail*.

Critical Thinking

In a small group discuss why voting is important and how people find out about candidates. Then, discuss the ways Mrs. Sanchez reached voters. Discuss why Luis and his mother were often surrounded by reporters. Then answer these questions.

- How do you think people decide who to vote for in an election?

- How do reporters help people make voting decisions?

Why Is Voting IMPORTANT?

Voting gives people the **opportunity** to tell the government what is important to them. The government affects everyone—even you. People in government decide how to manage the water you drink and the parks where you play. They protect the quality of the air you breathe.

The government decides the **approximate** number of police and fire officials your town needs.

When people vote, they decide if they **approve** of the job the government is doing or not.

Register to vote when you turn eighteen! All you have to do is fill out a form and send it in by the **deadline**. Then you can **announce** how you feel to the government!

Structured Vocabulary Discussion

When your teacher says a vocabulary word, you and your partner should each write down the first words you think of on a piece of paper. When your teacher says "Stop," exchange papers with your partner and explain the words on your lists.

Throughout the week, add to your vocabulary journal entries. Record new insights and other words that relate to this week's vocabulary.

Picture It

Copy this word web in your vocabulary journal. Fill in the empty circles with the kind of information that people **announce**.

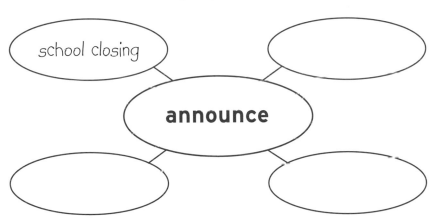

Copy this chart into your vocabulary journal. Fill in each space with an activity that your parents would **approve**.

approve

doing homework

PRESS OUT CIRCLED CROSS(ES) ⊕ TO VOTE
VOTER DETACH AND KEEP THIS STUB.   11/02/04

MECKLENBURG COUNTY
SEPARATE VOTE
PRESIDENT / VICE PRESIDENT
(YOU MAY VOTE FOR ONE)
                                    DEM ➤   +
JOHN F. KERRY/JOHN EDWARDS   REP ➤   +
GEORGE W. BUSH/DICK CHENEY
MICHAEL BADNARIK/RICHARD CAMPAGNA LIB ➤
                                          ➤   +
WRITE-IN
STRAIGHT PARTY VOTE
(YOU MAY VOTE FOR ONE)
                                          ➤   +
                                          ➤   +

A 2004 Election Ballot

The People of Colorado . . .

by Katherine Mackin

We are swept into a sea of color,
swimming in red, white, and blue.
Streamers, balloons, and confetti
rain from the ceiling as my father
and everyone else cheers.
The gavel bangs on the podium,
the starting bell in a great race.
Then we hear the announcement
roar through the arena—
Welcome to the Convention!

The convention floor is a forest
of people, politicians, and posters.
I stand on my seat so I can see the action.
It is time to hear the nominations for
the president of the United States.
Here goes Alabama. There goes Alaska.
Finally it is our state's opportunity to speak.
My father steps to the microphone,
his voice a low, rumbling thunder, and says—
The people of Colorado nominate . . .

CLOSE CALLS IN VOTING HISTORY

Sometimes voters feel like they are powerless. But one vote can make a big difference. Read this list of close calls in voting history.

★ 1867 ★

The United States bought the territory of Alaska. The decision narrowly passed in the U.S. Senate. We could have missed out on having this wonderful state as part of our country.

★ 1948 ★

Harry S. Truman was elected president. His opponent was Thomas Dewey. Dewey needed only one more vote in each district of Ohio and California for a tie. Then the House of Representatives would have decided the election.

★ 1960 ★

Richard Nixon lost the presidential election. He needed only one more vote in each district of four states to win. John F. Kennedy was elected instead. A few more voters found President Kennedy the more likable candidate.

★ 1977 ★

Albert H. Wheeler was elected mayor of Ann Arbor, Michigan by one vote—10,660 to 10,659. He was grateful for that one vote.

President Truman's win over Dewey was a surprise to everyone—including newspaper writers!

President Kennedy signs a bill honoring Frederick Douglass.

Suffixes -*ful*, -*able*, and -*less*

Former President Ronald Reagan

Activity One

Suffixes -*ful*, -*able*, and -*less*

A suffix is a word part found at the end of some words. It changes the meaning of the root word. The suffix -*ful* means "full of." The suffix -*able* means "able to," and the suffix -*less* means "not having" or "without." Here are some words with suffixes -*ful*, -*able*, and -*less*: *hopeful, cheerful, unbelievable, enjoyable, fearless, hopeless*. Listen for these suffixes as your teacher reads *Close Calls in Voting History*.

Suffixes -*ful*, -*able*, and -*less* in Context

In small groups, read *Close Calls in Voting History* and make a list of all the words with the suffixes -*ful*, -*able*, and -*less*. Discuss the meaning of these words based on the root word and suffix.

Activity Two

peace	use
help	read
thought	color

Explore Words Together

With a partner, add the suffix -*ful*, -*able*, or -*less* to each of the words on the right. Make a list of the new words and be ready to share their definitions with the class.

Activity Three

Explore Words in Writing

With a partner, make a list of words with the suffixes -*ful*, -*able*, or -*less*. Write a sentence using a root word from the list. Then have your partner rewrite the sentence adding a suffix to the root word. Discuss the words you wrote.

How to Run for Office... and Win!

by Sol Murray

Do you think you have what it takes to win an election? Maybe you'll want to be class president in a few years. If you want to be elected to any office, you'll have to start a campaign. A campaign is the process you go through to get people to vote for you. You will tell voters about yourself and persuade them to vote for you.

No matter how big or how small the office, it's important to run a good, acceptable campaign!

What strategy could you use to help you figure out the word "office"?

Win with KIM!

VOTE

Get Started!

Think about why people should vote for you. Answer these questions for yourself.

- What makes you a dependable leader?
- Can you show that you are truthful?
- How do you want to help your school and classmates?

Next, place your name on the ballot. A ballot is a list of the names of people to vote for in an election.

Select Your Team

You will need a campaign team, or staff, to do different jobs. For example, a member of your team can help you write speeches. Others can design posters, fliers, and buttons. Approve everything your staff does because your name is on the ballot!

What strategies could you use to help you understand the information on this page?

437

Decide on Your Issues

If you can show the voters that you understand what they want, you will have a successful campaign. Talk to students about their concerns and thoughts. Then write a list of issues. The list might include some of the following ideas.

- Build a community garden at your school.
- Raise money for school programs.
- Build school spirit: Write a school song or design a new mascot.

Create Your Campaign Image

Choose two or three issues and make a plan about how you will meet each goal. Use words from your plan to make campaign posters. Come up with a catchy sentence or phrase that your classmates will remember.

Partner Jigsaw Technique Read a section of the procedural essay with a partner and write down one strategy to help you monitor your understanding. Be prepared to summarize your section and share one strategy.

What issues do you think students would like to vote on at your school?

"I LIKE IKE"

Dwight Eisenhower's nickname was Ike. In 1952, his campaign slogan was "I Like Ike." And people liked it. He was elected president of the United States.

VOTE

Get the Word Out

Use posters, fliers, and buttons to get your message out to the voters. Plan events to talk about your ideas. Meet with people after school or at lunch. Talk about the election and what you want to do as a leader. This will help you figure out the approximate number of students who may vote for you.

Were any parts of this page difficult to understand? What strategies could you use to help you understand what you are reading?

Stay on Your Toes

Be prepared to answer questions about your ideas. Students may ask you why they should vote for you and not the other candidate. When you answer, be fair and honest. You can talk about how your goals are different or even the same as your opponent's. Keep your message hopeful. People like to vote for positive candidates.

make the RIGHT choice!

ELECTION!

SUGGESTION BOX

Election Day Speech

Election day is here. If you win, you may give a speech. This is a way to say that you are grateful to all the voters! If you lose, you may say thank you to your staff for their help. Here are steps to prepare for your speech.

Prepare. Plan your message. If you won, talk about the work ahead. If you lost, talk about how you hope the school will be a better place anyway. Write the main points of your speech on index cards.

Practice. Read your speech out loud. Do this several times in front of your friends or parents. Speak slowly to avoid sounding nervous or breathless.

Poise. Stand up straight and keep your hands out of your pockets. Look at the people in the audience. Smile! You've worked really hard!

How can strategic reading help you understand the information on this page? Explain.

WASHINGTON

George Washington gave the shortest inaugural speech ever, the second time he was elected. It was only 135 words!

Think and Respond

Reflect and Write

- You and your partner have read a section of *How to Run for Office*. Discuss with your partner the difficulties you had and the strategies you used to understand.

- On one side of an index card, write the name of the section you read. On the other side, write the strategy you used to help you understand. Then, discuss strategies with a pair that read a different section.

Suffixes *-ful*, *-able*, and *-less* in Context

Search through *How to Run for Office* and list the words that have the suffixes *-ful*, *-able*, and *-less*. Write a list of the words you find. With a partner, discuss how the suffix changes the meaning of each base word.

Turn and Talk

MONITOR UNDERSTANDING: STRATEGIC READING

Discuss with a partner what you have learned about using strategies to help you understand difficult passages.

- How does strategic reading help you monitor your understanding?

With a partner, read page 437 again. Discuss the strategies you could use to help monitor your understanding of this page.

Critical Thinking

With a partner, discuss the suggestions in *How to Run for Office* for running a campaign. Then answer these questions.

- What issues would you choose if you ran for class president?

- How could giving a speech help you get support for your ideas?

First Landing Jump, 1961
Robert Rauschenberg (1925–present)

UNIT: Our Valuable Earth

| THEME | 15 | Precious Resources |

| THEME | 16 | Recycle and Renew |

Viewing

This artwork was created out of many different materials. The artist is famous for creating works that he calls "combines." The artist finds objects and recycles them to make his "combine" art.

1. What different kinds of objects and materials do you see in this "combine" piece of art?

2. What new ideas does this art give you about using resources other than paint and brushes to create art?

3. Have you ever created or seen artwork made by reusing materials? How is it similar to or different from this artwork?

4. What do you think would have happened to these materials if the artist had not collected them?

In This UNIT

In this unit, you will read about our renewable and nonrenewable resources. You will also read about how you can reuse and recycle to save Earth's resources.

Contents

Precious Resources

RACHEL
The Story of Rachel Carson

BY AMY EHRLICH

ILLUSTRATED BY WENDELL MINOR

Critical Listening

Critical listening means listening for facts and opinions. Listen to the focus questions your teacher will read to you.

IT'S ARBOR DAY!

Join friends and neighbors for Arbor Day this Saturday at Centertown Park!

Why do we celebrate Arbor Day? It is no **mystery**. People love trees. We plant trees on this day and discuss ways to **preserve** them. Everyone wants the **privilege** of enjoying trees in the future.

It all started in the 1870s when J. Sterling Morton, a man from Nebraska, called on neighbors to plant trees. This idea caught on with folks on the treeless plains of Nebraska. Soon, with **irrigation**, the people were able to **cultivate** trees across Nebraska.

Trees give shade from the sun. Trees also help to keep soil in place. Join the fun and plant a tree this Saturday!

Structured Vocabulary Discussion

In a small group, review all your vocabulary words. Then classify the words into two categories: words that name things and words that show action. Share your ideas with another group and discuss why each word belongs in its category.

Throughout the week, add to your vocabulary journal entries. Record new insights and other words that relate to this week's vocabulary.

Picture It

Copy this word web into your vocabulary journal. Name things you try to **preserve**.

preserve

friends

Copy this chart into your vocabulary journal. Fill in the columns with examples of a **privilege** you have at home, at school, and in your community.

privilege		
at home	**at school**	**in my community**
I can use the phone to talk to friends.		

Use Fix-up Strategies
Decoding and Word Analysis

LETTER SOUNDS and **WORD PARTS** can help you figure out a new word.

Stuck on Word → **Word Attack**

Use what you know about letter sounds and word parts to figure out a new word.

TURN AND TALK Listen as your teacher reads from *Rachel: The Story of Rachel Carson* and models how to use fix-up strategies by using letter sounds and word parts. Then discuss answers to these questions.

• Did you hear any word in the text that you did not understand?

• How would you use letter sounds or word parts to help you understand the word?

TAKE IT WITH YOU Fix-up strategies, such as letter sounds and word parts, will help you figure out the meaning of a word. First sound out the word. If you have never heard the word, look at word parts, such as endings. They may give you a clue about the word's meaning. Use a chart like the one below to help you.

Word I Got Stuck On	What I Did				Which One Worked?
	Used Illustrations	Used Phonics	Read On	Broke It into Parts	
widened	✔	✔	✔	✔	First I sounded out the word. I heard the word wide in "widened." I know wide means "the length from side to side."

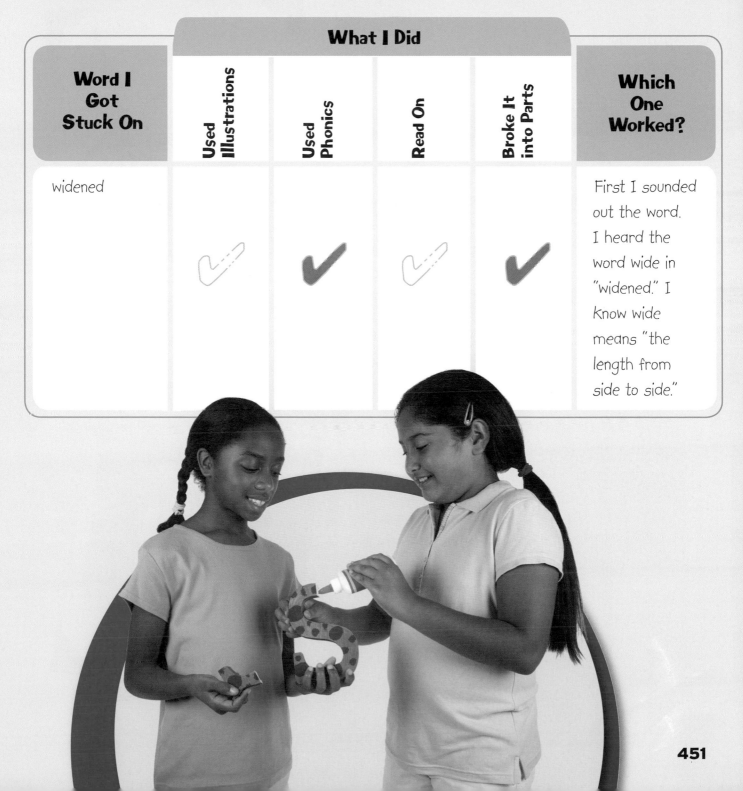

My Fishing Diary

by Clyde Wolf

Saturday, June 3

Dear Diary,

This morning Dad and I watched the sun rise from his lobster boat. Usually spending a whole day with Dad makes up for waking so early. But today was not a day for fun. Most of our lobster traps were empty.

Dad was worried. He thinks we have few lobsters in our traps because of over-fishing. Too many people fishing means there may not be enough lobsters for Dad to catch this season.

Sunday, June 4

Dear Diary,

We had more disappointment today. Dad caught a few big lobsters, but they were all females with eggs. Lobsters with eggs must be marked and tossed back. This helps keep the right number of lobsters in the bay.

Dad talked with other fishermen. They all had good days. Maybe the problem is not over-fishing after all. I said we should try using different bait.

Saturday, June 10

Dear Diary,

This morning was cloudy. Then it started to rain. The rain got our attention but it did not ruin our good mood. Almost all our traps were full! The new lobster bait seemed to work. Each time we pulled up a trap, it was my job to put rubber bands on the lobsters' claws. This way the lobsters couldn't pinch us. By the end of the day, we had lots of lobsters to sell.

Sunday, June 11

Dear Diary,

Today was even better than yesterday. My fingers were rough from banding so many lobsters. I was glad when it was time to quit! After supper, Dad gave me credit for turning things around. He reminded me that it was my idea to take action. I think the nice feeling of fullness I had tonight was as much from happiness as from the ice cream dessert!

Word Study

PREHISTORIC Power

Did you know that the oil we use today to fuel cars and heat our homes is millions of years old? We use this crude oil much faster than any new oil can be created. That is why crude oil is called a *nonrenewable resource*. We cannot replace or renew it.

Read on for an explanation of how crude oil forms.

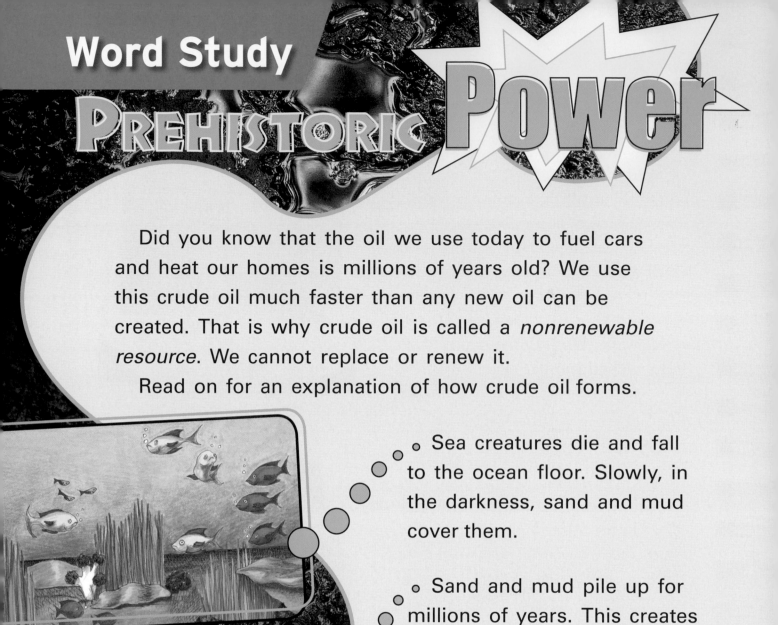

Sea creatures die and fall to the ocean floor. Slowly, in the darkness, sand and mud cover them.

Sand and mud pile up for millions of years. This creates heat and pressure. This action turns the bodies of sea creatures below into oil.

The discovery of crude oil causes excitement. Often, oil is found in wilderness areas. Pumping the oil up from the ground disturbs plants and animals. This is why people must balance the protection of nature with the need for oil.

454

Suffixes *-ness*, *-ment*, *-ion*, and *-tion*

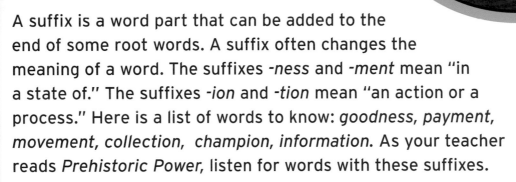

Oil Rig Platform

Activity One

About Suffixes *-ness*, *-ment*, *-ion*, and *-tion*

A suffix is a word part that can be added to the end of some root words. A suffix often changes the meaning of a word. The suffixes *-ness* and *-ment* mean "in a state of." The suffixes *-ion* and *-tion* mean "an action or a process." Here is a list of words to know: *goodness, payment, movement, collection, champion, information.* As your teacher reads *Prehistoric Power,* listen for words with these suffixes.

Suffixes *-ness*, *-ment*, *-ion* and *-tion* in Context

With a partner, read *Prehistoric Power*. Make a list of the words with the suffixes *-ness*, *-ment*, *-ion*, and *-tion*. Discuss how the suffix in each word helps you understand its meaning.

Activity Two

Explore Words Together

Add the suffixes *-ness*, *-ment*, *-ion*, or *-tion* to the words at right and list them. Ask a partner to explain the meaning of each word you made.

kind	disappoint
predict	correct
amaze	eager

Activity Three

Explore Words in Writing

With a partner, list other words that have the suffixes *-ness*, *-ment*, *-ion*, and *-tion*. Talk about what each word means with the suffix and without it. Use each in a sentence. Choose two to share with the class.

RACING with the Sun

by Richard King

The North American Solar Challenge is a competition to design cars and race them from Texas to Canada. But these are not ordinary cars. They do not run on gasoline. All the cars in the race are powered by energy from the sun! I work for the Department of Energy. I am keeping a journal of the race. My journal will tell all about these cars and the talented people who race them.

Topeka, Kansas, May 16

Today I met some of the teams that will be racing. I also got to see their new cars for the first time. This year there will be teams from 20 colleges and universities. Students have spent the last two years building their cars. I stare in amazement at the designs. What can these cars achieve? I'll soon find out.

What strategy can help you figure out the word *amazement* if you do not know it?

Solar Car Team

The Race Begins!

Austin, Texas, July 17

And they're off! Today the race began. Despite some clouds, the race start was great. Thousands cheered as the cars left on the longest cross-country solar car race ever. The goal is to reach the finish line in Calgary, Canada faster than anyone else. The cars must use only sunlight for fuel!

Weatherford, Texas, July 18

The excitement is growing. Starting today, each team must try to drive as far as it can for several days in a row. Yesterday was easy. Each team drove 212 miles in four to six hours. Many cars had energy left to drive even farther. Today, teams begin the part of the race that is more than 2000 miles long. Teams will drive as far as they can in 10 hours each day. This will really test each car's ability to use energy from the sun.

What words on this page are new to you? What strategies helped you figure them out?

Along the race route, July 19

It was cloudy and raining this morning. The race leaders tried to speed ahead of the clouds, but they couldn't. When there are clouds, batteries lose energy and cars slow down. The top three cars had to stop to charge their batteries. Team members had to be careful not to damage their cars as they worked in the rain. As the leaders parked by the side of the road, five other teams passed them!

Say Something Technique
Take turns reading a section of text, covering it up, and then saying something about it to your partner. You may say any thought or idea that the text brings to your mind.

Crossing into Canada, July 21

This race turns students into experts about energy. They must pay attention to their cars and to the weather. Teams must decide how to save energy when the sun is not shining. To power a solar car all day, day after day, is very hard. But the teams are showing that energy from the sun really works.

Why do you think the teams are racing cars which run on energy from the sun?

Solar Car on the Road

Racing through Canada, July 23

Today I was really impressed with the University of California team. This team is amazing to watch when they have a problem. Everyone jumps into action, and they all work together. Before they are finished, someone with a list calls out each item to make sure nothing has been forgotten. Then the car is right back in the race!

No team will win just from teamwork. The team's car must be powerful. The more power a car has, the faster it will go. The most important part of a solar car is the collection of cells on the car's roof. These cells change sunlight into electricity. The better the cells are at doing this, the faster the car will go. Under sunny skies, a good solar car travels about the same speed as a normal car.

> How can using word parts help you understand the meanings of "teamwork" and "powerful"? Explain.

Another Solar Car Team

Calgary, Canada, July 27

This great race came to an exciting finish today in Calgary! The University of Michigan and University of Minnesota were ahead of the other cars this morning. For a while they were even next to each other. Then Minnesota fell behind Michigan. But the competition wasn't over! Later, Michigan had to stop to fix something. But they stayed in the lead. Finally, Michigan crossed the finish line just 11 minutes ahead of Minnesota! The team from Michigan is the champion!

Tomorrow there will be a big party for all the teams. Teams will receive awards for teamwork, creativity, fairness, and best new team. In my mind, all the teams are winners!

What word on this page did you sound out to help learn its meaning? Explain.

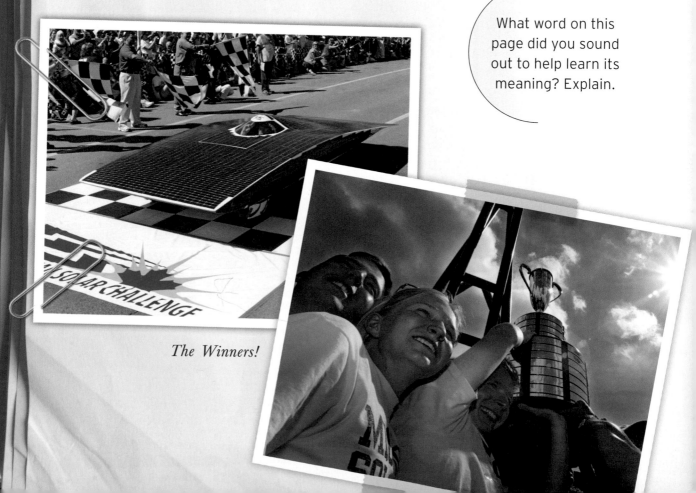

The Winners!

Think and Respond

Reflect and Write

- As you read sections of *Racing with the Sun*, you and your partner shared your thoughts and ideas. Discuss these thoughts and ideas with your partner.

- Talk about any words you did not know as you read. On one side of an index card, write a word you did not know. On the other side, write the strategy you used to figure out the meaning.

Suffixes *-ness*, *-ment*, *-ion*, and *-tion* in Context

Search through *Racing with the Sun* for words with suffixes *-ness*, *-ment*, *-ion*, and *-tion*. Make a list of your words. Then choose three of the words. Write a sentence about being careful with resources with each word.

Turn and Talk

USE FIX-UP STRATEGIES: DECODING AND WORD ANALYSIS

Discuss with a partner what you have learned so far about using fix-up strategies such as decoding and word analysis.

- How can using letter sounds and word parts help you figure out a word's meaning?

Look back at page 460. With your partner, discuss what strategies you would use to help a classmate understand the word *creativity*.

Critical Thinking

With a group, brainstorm ways the cars in *Racing with the Sun* are different from other cars. List ways a solar car might be better than other cars and ways it might not be better. Then answer these questions.

- What might be difficult about driving a solar car?

- How can solar cars help the environment?

Sunshine Schools

Some schools are letting the sunshine in! "Daylit schools" use the sun's power to light classrooms. On most days, direct sunlight is **adequate**. Sometimes the sky is dark. Then the school uses stored solar energy to power the classroom's lights.

This is a big change. Most schools use electric lights. More than half of this electricity comes from burning coal. But burning coal can **damage** the environment. It causes air pollution.Using **renewable** solar energy can help **diminish** pollution.

There may be other benefits as well. Some people believe students **achieve** more at daylit schools. They may score better on tests.

Perhaps in the future all schools will let the sunshine in!

Burning Coal

Solar Panel

Structured Vocabulary Discussion

Work in a small group to find the word that fits in the sentence. Be sure you can explain how the words in each sentence are related.

Subtract is to *add* as _____ is to *increase*.

Score is to *win* as _____ is to *success*.

Stop is to *nonstop* as _____ is to *nonrenewable*.

Throughout the week, add to your vocabulary journal entries. Record new insights and other words that relate to this week's vocabulary.

Picture It

Copy this word wheel into your vocabulary journal. Fill in the spaces with words or phrases that **renewable** makes you think of.

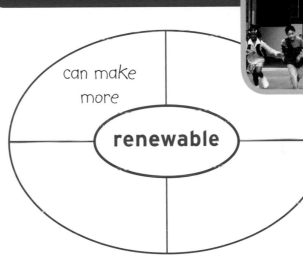

can make more

renewable

Copy this word web into your vocabulary journal. Fill in the empty circles with things you would like to **achieve**.

win spelling bee

achieve

Blow, Wind, Blow!

Today, *Miller* is a common last name. But long ago, *miller* was also the name for a common job. Millers used windmills as the power to grind grain into flour. A windmill is a machine that runs on energy from the wind. If wind power wasn't adequate, millers could not grind flour easily. That meant people might not have flour for bread. Wind power and millers were important to many people.

Traditional Song

Blow, wind, blow.

And go, mill, go!

That the Miller may grind his corn;

That the Baker may take it,

And into bread make it,

And bring us a loaf in the morn.

Blow wind, blow.

And go, mill, go.

That the Miller may grind his wheat;

That the Baker may deal

To the Miller at his meal

A delicious and yummy treat!

Make WORMS Work for You!

Dear Gardener,

Did you know that worms can make your garden grow beautifully? Our company, Wormworks, can help.

As worms quietly dig tunnels in the soil, they create paths for air and water to flow underground. These paths help plant roots get what they need. After worms eat, they leave waste behind. This waste, called *castings*, helps plants grow healthy and strong.

Add soil to a large box with holes in it for air. The friendly folks at Wormworks will carefully deliver worms right to your box. Each week, add food scraps to the soil. In time, you will have wonderfully rich soil ready for your garden!

Sincerely,

Walter "Wormy" Wentword
Head Worm Wrangler
Wormworks

Suffixes *-ly* and *-fully*

Activity One

About Suffixes *-ly* and *-fully*

A *suffix* is a group of letters added to the end of a root word to form a new word. The suffix *-ly* means "the way something is done." The suffix *-fully* adds the meaning "with." Here are some words that have the suffixes *-ly* and *-fully*: *clearly, closely, neatly, softly, happily, carefully, joyfully, truthfully*. As your teacher reads *Make Worms Work for You!* listen for words with suffixes *-ly* and *-fully*.

Suffixes *-ly* and *-fully* in Context

With a partner, read *Make Worms Work for You!* Search for words with the endings *-ly* and *-fully*. List the words and circle the ending in each word.

Activity Two

Explore Words Together

Review suffixes with a partner. Then look at the words listed on the right. Write the root word for each word. For example, the root word of *hopefully* is *hope*. Discuss how the suffix changes the meaning of the word.

hopefully	calmly
respectfully	clearly
easily	fearfully

Activity Three

Explore Words in Writing

With a partner, write sentences about different natural resources. First, write a sentence with a word that has the suffix *-ly* or *-fully*. Then your partner writes a sentence using the root word of your suffix word. Switch roles.

THE LAZY, LAZY HARE

A FOLKTALE FROM NIGERIA

retold by Maryann Macdonald

Never had it been so hot and dry. Every day the animals in the wilderness looked at the sky hopefully for signs of rain. No rain came. Instead, the sun blazed down. How could they live without water to drink?

One evening, after the sun slipped behind a faraway mountain, the animals gathered together. They wanted to discuss the problem. "Hippo and Alligator have already left the wilderness," said Baboon. "Soon the rest of us will have to leave, too. We cannot stay here without water." Baboon's statement made the animals sad. No one wanted to leave home.

> What details help you create a mental image of the animals as they look to the sky for rain?

468

Calmly, Old Tortoise came forward. "Long ago, when the sun burned as hot as it is today, we animals found water deep under the earth." He tapped the ground with his foot. "I know there is water under the ground here, and it is renewable. We must dig deep and find it."

The animals' fear and sadness began to diminish. Elephant had a good memory. He remembered a place where there had once been a well. The animals decided to dig there the next morning.

At dawn, the digging began. Aardvark sharpened his claws and helpfully broke up the clay. Rhino used his powerful feet to kick away soil and rocks. Even Snake slithered over and wrapped her long body around plant roots to help pull them out.

Hare sat hidden behind a large rock. He watched everyone working in the hot sun. "I wish they would hurry up," he thought. "I am so thirsty!"

What information on this page helped you create a new mental image of the animals?

469

At last, the animals struck water! Each animal took a drink of the cool, clear water. Tortoise was last. Then, just as he took his first delicious sip . . . BOOM! From behind a bush, Hare began pounding on a drum with a big stick. Frightened by the awful noise, the animals all ran away.

Alone at last, Hare hopped over to the waterhole. He slurped up the cool, clear water greedily until his stomach swelled like a pumpkin. Then he dove in. He swam and splashed. He washed his dirty feet and scrubbed inside his pointy ears. Then, cool, comfortable, and clean, Hare hopped happily away.

Reverse Think-Aloud Technique
Listen as your partner reads part of the text aloud. Choose a point in the text to stop your partner and ask what he or she is thinking about the text at the moment. Then switch roles with your partner.

How has your picture of Hare changed as you read?

The animals returned to the water hole the next morning. They discovered their cool, clear water was now muddy! Lion roared angrily. He pointed to Hare's footprints.

How has your picture of the animals at the water hole changed after reading this page?

"Hare was too lazy to help us dig. But he was not too lazy to drink our water and get it dirty! We need to teach him a lesson."

"I have an idea," said Old Tortoise, smiling. He whispered it to his friends.

"Hare will be sorry now," said Bush Fowl, and everyone nodded in agreement. Together, they gathered the stickiest tree sap they could find. They piled the dark sap in front of the waterhole. Monkey carefully built the figure of a strange-looking animal out of the sap. Then all the animals hid behind the big rock. There they waited for Hare to sneak back to the waterhole for another drink.

Finally, Hare arrived. "Hello," he called out to the animal. It did not answer. He tapped it on the shoulder. The sticky sap trapped his foot. Soon all four of his feet were stuck in the sticky sap. He was trapped! "Help!" he cried to the other animals. "Come free your poor brother!" Hare kicked mightily against the sap.

"You are no brother of ours!" shouted the animals, jumping out from behind the rock.

"You are a thief," said Baboon. "You were too lazy to help us and you stole our water."

Old Tortoise came forward. "We will free you, Hare," he said, "but leave now and don't ever come back." Lion roared his approval. Hyena showed her sharp teeth. Hastily, Hare ran away as fast as he could and was never seen again in this part of the wilderness.

What details here show Hare's fear? How do these details help you form a picture in your mind?

Think and Respond

Reflect and Write

- You and your partner have read *The Lazy, Lazy Hare*. Discuss your thoughts and ideas the two of you shared as you read.

- On one side of an index card, write a mental image you had as the story began. On the other side, write how this mental image changed as you read further. Discuss your choices with your partner.

Suffixes *-ly* and *-fully* in Context

Search through *The Lazy, Lazy Hare* for words with the suffixes *-ly*, and *-fully*. Make a list of your words and compare this list with a partner's.

Turn and Talk

CREATE IMAGES: REVISE

Discuss what you have learned about revising mental images as you read.

- How do your mental images change as you read?

With a partner, look at page 470. Talk about your mental image of Hare at the water hole on this page. Describe how your image of Hare changed as you finished reading the story.

Critical Thinking

With a partner, talk about how water is an important resource in *The Lazy, Lazy Hare*. Discuss how water sources are important to plants, animals, and people where you live. Then answer these questions.

- What would happen if this water became polluted or dried up?

- How can you protect water sources for the future?

Recycle and Renew

Contents

Modeled Reading

Shared Reading

Interactive Reading

JUST A DREAM

by Chris Van Allsburg

Appreciative Listening

Appreciative listening means listening for language that helps you create a picture in your mind. Listen to the focus questions your teacher will read to you.

Ask the Recyclopedia!

Hi, I'm the Recyclopedia! I can answer all your questions about the three Rs: Reduce, Reuse, and **Recycle**. Ask me some questions!

What does it mean to reduce?

When you reduce, you use less of something. We use **enormous** amounts of energy resources every day. You can help reduce the demand for energy. Turn off the lights when you leave a room. Take a shorter shower or bath.

What's the difference between reusing and recycling?

Reusing means to use something more than once. Many common things are **reusable**. For example, you can use a milk jug to store your things.

Recycling means to turn an old object into a new one. You can recycle a can. Do not **dispose** of it in a trashcan. Toss it in a special bin. Later machines will shred it and melt it. The can will appear in the **future** as something new.

dispose   reusable   enormous   recycle   future

Structured Vocabulary Discussion

When your teacher says a vocabulary word, you and your partner should each write on a piece of paper the first words you think of. When your teacher says, "Stop," exchange papers with your partner and explain to each other any of the words on your lists.

Throughout the week, add to your vocabulary journal entries. Record new insights and other words that relate to this week's vocabulary.

Picture It

Copy the following chart into your vocabulary journal. List items that are **reusable** and items that are not reusable.

reusable	not reusable
cloth napkins	paper towels

Copy this word web into your vocabulary journal. Complete the word web with items you can **recycle**.

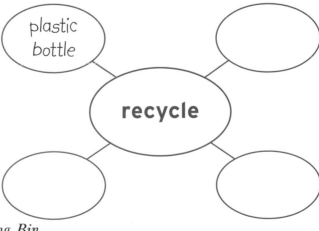

plastic bottle

recycle

Recycling Bin

Determine Importance

Purpose for Reading

Information can be **IMPORTANT** or not important based on why you are reading.

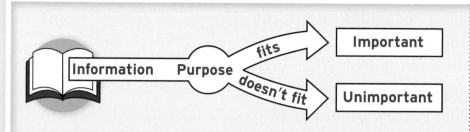

Decide whether information is important or not based on your purpose for reading.

TURN AND TALK Listen as your teacher reads from *Just a Dream* and models how to determine importance. Discuss with a partner answers to the following questions.

- What information did you notice?

- How did your purpose for reading help you decide if the information was important or unimportant?

TAKE IT WITH YOU Next time you read a selection, think about why you are reading it. Your purpose for reading will help you decide if the information you notice is important or unimportant. Your purpose for reading may change as you notice new information. Use a chart like the one below to help you decide what is important.

Information That I Noticed	My Purpose for Reading Tells Me It Is...
I noticed that Walter dumped all the trash into one bin.	✔ **Important** ☐ **Unimportant**
I noticed that Walter liked to watch television.	☐ **Important** ✔ **Unimportant**

LETTERS to the Editor

Big Stink over Garbage Barges

May 1, 2007

Dear Editor,

I think we can all agree on a few things about trash. It is clogging up our streets. It pollutes our air. Now the question is: How can we get rid of it?

There is only one solution that makes sense to me. Ship it off! The city's trash should be placed on the big boats called "garbage barges." Then it could be shipped far away. It can be burned at a garbage plant in another state.

We should not put our trash in landfills. These are harmful to the environment. And who wants these dumps smelling up our neighborhoods? Not me! Do you?

Sincerely,

Cecily Slocum

The Ugly Truth About Trash

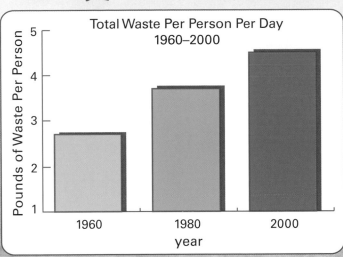

Total Waste Per Person Per Day 1960–2000

May 1, 2007

Dear Editor,

Does anyone remember what happened in 1987? A garbage barge called the Mobro 4000 traveled 6,000 miles. It was shopping for a place to dump the garbage from New York City. Six states and three countries turned away the trash. Finally, the barge returned to New York and the trash was burned.

Do we want this to happen again? No! We need to develop better recycling programs instead. We need to have workshops for citizens to learn more about recycling and the environment.

It is up to us to protect our environment before it's too late.

Sincerely,

Sanjay Akbar

COMPOSTING!

A Trashy Trick

Instead of throwing away kitchen waste, try composting. Composting recycles things like fruit and vegetable peels, dead leaves, and grass clippings. Nature breaks down the materials into new soil. Here's how to make your own compost pile.

1. Use an old garbage can with a tight-fitting lid. Have someone punch holes in the side. Keep the can in a shady spot.

2. Put in leftovers from chopped or shredded fruits and vegetables, as well as table scraps. Do not include meat or milk products. Add trimmings from garden plants.

3. Spray the contents with water. Get it damp but not runny.

4. Every week, roll the can to mix the garbage. In about a month, the compost will be ready to use in your garden.

Consonant Doubling

Activity One

About Consonant Doubling

Some root words, such as *pop*, have a consonant-vowel-consonant pattern. When you add an ending to these words, double the final consonant before adding the ending. Here are some words with double consonants before the ending: *big/bigger, drop/dropping, hug/hugged, wet/wetter, sun/sunny, sit/sitting*. As your teacher reads *Composting! A Trashy Trick*, listen for words that have the final consonant doubled before the ending.

Consonant Doubling in Context

With a partner, read back through *Composting! A Trashy Trick* to find words in which the final consonant before the ending is doubled. Make a list of the words you find.

Activity Two

Explore Words Together

get	stir
fit	stop
chip	hot

Work with a partner to add endings to the words on the right. Be sure the ending you add makes a real word. Don't forget to double the final consonants. Exchange your list with another partner team's and compare words.

Activity Three

Explore Words in Writing

Write sentences that describe compost piles. Use words that double the final consonant before the endings. Exchange your sentences with a partner. Circle all the words with doubled final consonants.

Scrappy Steve

by Margaret Fetty

Steve Watkins stared at the poster of a soldier holding a crying boy. The words on the poster read, "We can't all go—but we can all help!"

Steve knew exactly how that boy felt. Steve's dad had joined the army in 1943. He had been gone a year. While Steve felt proud, he missed his dad.

As Steve turned, he saw Mrs. Riley lugging a stack of newspapers. Janie, her daughter, skipped behind. Janie held a paper in each hand.

"That looks heavy!" said Steve, grabbing some of the papers.

What important information do you notice on this page? Explain.

29¢

We can't all go—
but we can all help!

"Thanks, Steve," said Mrs. Riley. "I'm taking them to the courthouse. The newspaper said the town was having a scrap drive. Factories will recycle this paper into shipping packages that go to the soldiers. This is one way I can help!"

"I'm helping, too!" added Janie, holding up her newspapers.

At the courthouse, three big trucks were parked out in front. One had piles of newspapers, and another had stacks of rubber tires. A third truck had an assortment of metal pans, tire rims, and rusty tools. A bin held screws and nails. Mrs. Riley explained that the rubber scrap would be recycled into new jeep tires, while the metal scrap would become airplanes.

How does your purpose for reading help you decide what is important information on this page?

Steve thought about how his dad, Mrs. Riley, and Janie were helping the country. He wanted to help, too. But how?

Steve was still deep in thought when he got home. His mother was in the kitchen chopping vegetables for a stew.

Like many other women, Mrs. Watkins was working in a factory to help her country. With so many men in the service, the factories needed workers.

Steve went into the living room and sat in front of the big radio. He switched on the radio just as his favorite announcer said, "Use it up and wear it out. Make it do, or do without! And don't forget to give to your local scrap drives."

Two-Word Technique
Write down two words that reflect your thoughts about each page. Discuss them with your partner.

Is the information about a scrap drive important or unimportant information? How can you decide?

Steve tapped his fingers and looked out the window at the shed in the backyard.

"I have a swell idea," exclaimed Steve. He loaded his wagon up with old metal parts from the shed.

"Mom, the town is collecting scrap metal to be recycled, so I'm taking these old things to the courthouse," Steve said.

Mrs. Watkins popped outside and added two pans on the pile.

Steve pulled the wagon down the sidewalk. His neighbor Mr. Thomas called out. "Where are you going with all that old metal?"

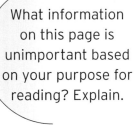

What information on this page is unimportant based on your purpose for reading? Explain.

"I'm helping our country!" Steve answered. "I'm taking it to be recycled."

"Would you take some old pipes for me?" Mr. Thomas asked.

As Steve tugged his heavy wagon, he got an idea. He would get his friends to gather scrap metal from their neighbors. They could help with the scrap drive!

The next day, Steve and his friends went from house to house asking people for scrap metal. They hauled old farm plows, wagon wheels, bikes, pots, cans, and fence railings. They even collected aluminum foil, lipstick tubes, and watches.

Mr. Camp, a reporter, saw Steve and his friends working. He offered to write a newspaper article to tell the community about Steve's scrap drive.

How does your purpose for reading help you determine what information on this page is important?

In the morning, Steve raced to get the newspaper. He read the headline happily—*Scrappy Steve Sorts Out Scrap.*

Mrs. Watkins walked into the kitchen and said, "I saw Mrs. Ruiz a minute ago. She wants to know if you can pick up some old washboards and irons."

"I'm on my way!" said Steve. He hopped up from the table, knowing that he was helping his country.

Think and Respond

Reflect and Write

- You and your partner have read parts of *Scrappy Steve* and written two words about each page. Discuss these words and your thoughts.

- On one side of an index card, write two words that best describe the story. On the other side, write how these words are related to your

Consonant Doubling in Context

Search through *Scrappy Steve* to find words that double the final consonant before an ending. Make a list of the words you find. Then write sentences about recycling using several of the words.

Turn and Talk

DETERMINE IMPORTANCE: PURPOSE FOR READING

Discuss with a partner what you have learned so far about how to determine importance based on your purpose for reading.

- How does your purpose for reading help you determine important information?

Look back at *Scrappy Steve*. Discuss with a partner how your purpose for reading helped you decide what is important information.

Critical Thinking

Discuss with your partner what the characters in *Scrappy Steve* did to recycle materials. Then answer these questions.

- Why is recycling important to the characters in the story?

- Do the characters in the story recycle the way we do today?

At Home with EARTH

Would you like to live in a house made of **litter**? Don't answer until you read about earth ships!

Earth ships are homes built with items that most people throw in the trash **bin**. The **assortment** of building materials includes cans, bottles, and tires. Believe it or not, these things can be used to build strong walls.

Earth ships are a form of **conservation**. They save resources by reusing products. Reusing these products prevents **pollution**, too.

Earth ships use sun and wind to make their own electricity. This saves oil and other resources. Many earth ships also collect rain and snow for water.

The walls of this earth ship were made by reusing old tires.

This earth ship has a large solar panel used to get power from the sun.

bin   litter   assortment   pollution   conservation

Structured Vocabulary Discussion

Write the vocabulary word that comes to mind for each of the following words or phrases that your teacher reads. Discuss your answers with a partner.

different kinds of toys in a store

factory with black smoke

leftover food along a road

Throughout the week, add to your vocabulary journal entries. Record new insights and other words that relate to this week's vocabulary.

Picture It

Copy this chart into your vocabulary journal. Fill in the rectangles with things that come in an **assortment**.

assortment

crayons	

Copy this word web into your vocabulary journal. Fill in the empty circles with kinds of **pollution**.

dirty stream

pollution

LESSONS
FROM A
LANDFILL

by Pauline Holihan

Garbage, trash, and litter
Like a mountain in the sky
Like a stinky, slimy critter.
How did this happen and why?

Could I be part of the cause?
I'd rather not say.
But give me a moment to think
If I hurt Earth today.

I got a bunch of plastic bags
At the grocery store.
Then I tossed them in the trash,
Did I hear the critter roar?

494

I threw out some pretty paper
After only scribbling a line.
If I had just used it more than once,
Then the critter would not be *mine*!

Then there's that can and bottle
That I put in the trash.
If I had put them in recycling tubs,
Then I could create a "critter mash!"

I helped create all this pollution,
Like a trash-generating machine.
If I had just stopped to recycle,
Then the Earth would be—Oh!—so clean.

Milk Carton Derby
REUSE AND RACE!

Seattle, WA—Wondering what to do with those old milk cartons? You might use them to make a boat. Then bring it to the Milk Carton Derby at the Seafair Festival on Saturday.

The Derby rules are simple. Make a boat that floats on used milk cartons or plastic milk containers. Only people can move the boats. Absolutely no engines are allowed. You also have to keep your boat above the water!

Milk Carton Derby races begin at 10 A.M. at Greenlake.

Syllables

Activity One

About Syllables

A syllable is a word part with a vowel sound. For example, the word *recycle* has three syllables: *re•cy•cle*. Here are examples of words with two syllables or more: *basket, dentist, napkin, window, music, paper, spider, student, dependent, bicycle, forgetful, communicate*. Listen for words with more than one syllable as your teacher reads *Milk Carton Derby*.

Syllables in Context

Read *Milk Carton Derby* with a partner. Together, find words with two, three, and four syllables. Make three lists of the words you find.

Activity Two

Explore Words Together

With a partner, read the words in the box to the right. Then, write the words and draw lines in each word to break the word into syllables.

garbage	conservation
pollution	litter
reuse	environment

Activity Three

Explore Words in Writing

Work with a partner to write several sentences about ways to reuse things that you might throw away. Try to use as many three- and four- syllable words as you can. When you are finished writing, exchange sentences with another partner team and count how many words with three and four syllables the other team used.

SPACE TRASH

by Peter Ernst

What's in space? Stars, planets, moons— and trash! Earth's trash problem doesn't stop on our planet's surface. For years, humans have been littering space, too.

Space trash is human-made objects that remain in space after they no longer have a useful purpose. These include nuts and bolts, shuttle parts, broken satellites, and old rockets.

Astronauts on the old Mir space station threw hundreds of objects into space. Most of these were in regular trash bags. So where did they all go?

How can letter sounds and word parts help you figure out the meaning of "satellite"?

What's the Big Deal?

Scientists say there are millions of pieces of trash flying around in space. Some space trash orbits Earth. You can even find trash on the surfaces of the moon, Venus, and Mars!

Space trash is dangerous. It can damage working satellites, space shuttles, and space stations. Space trash travels at 18,000 miles per hour. A four-inch piece of trash can have the same effect as twenty-five sticks of dynamite! A window on a spacecraft can be broken by a flake of paint.

> What is the meaning of "dangerous" on this page? Explain.

Can space junk fall from the sky? The answer is *yes*. But don't worry! You won't be hit on the head by a piece of space trash! Most items burn up as they get close to Earth. Other items fall into the ocean.

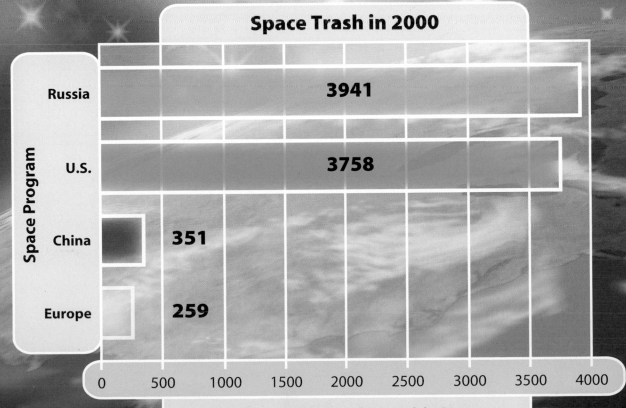

Space Trash in 2000

Space Program

Space Program	Number of Objects Left as Junk in Space
Russia	3941
U.S.	3758
China	351
Europe	259

Number of Objects Left as Junk in Space

(0 500 1000 1500 2000 2500 3000 3500 4000)

Famous Space Trash

A lot of space trash is just regular junk. But there are some pieces of space trash that could be in a museum.

The oldest piece of space trash is a satellite called the U.S. Vanguard. It was launched in 1958. It stopped working just six years later. That hunk of junk is still circling Earth today!

One famous piece of trash is clothing. The astronaut Edward White accidentally lost a glove in space. It happened during the first American space walk in 1965. The glove orbited Earth for a month. It finally burned up as it entered Earth's atmosphere.

Another famous piece of trash is a camera. Michael Collins lost it on a space walk in 1966. He was an astronaut on the *Gemini 10* mission. He had been taking pictures of the stars.

Reverse Think-Aloud Technique Listen as your partner reads part of the text aloud. Choose a point in the text to stop your partner and ask what he or she is thinking about the text at the moment. Then switch roles with your partner.

What fix-up strategies could you use to figure out the meaning of "astronaut"?

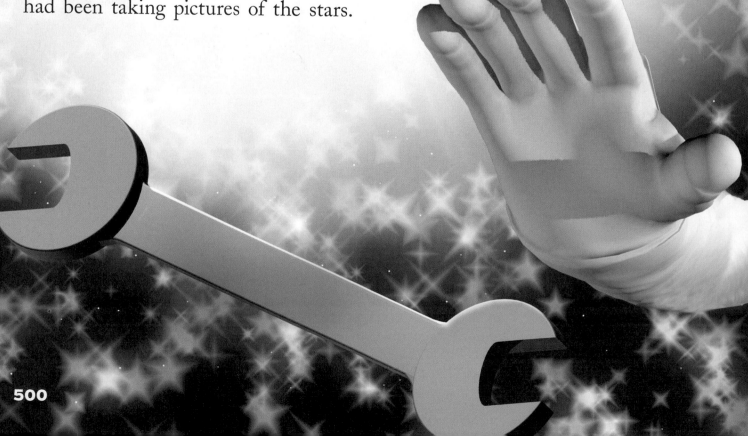

Space Station Trash

Did you know that there are people living in space right now? Astronauts have been at the International Space Station since 2000. We know that astronauts can't just throw their trash out the window. They have to conserve, reuse, and recycle.

Conservation is important on the space station. Anything that can be reused is. Almost ninety five percent of the water is recycled. But some waste can't be recycled. It must be crushed very small. This trash can leave the space station only when help arrives. One of the space station's "garbage trucks" has no crew. It is a spaceship controlled by people on Earth. When it gets to the space station, astronauts fill it with trash. They send it back to Earth's atmosphere. Then the whole ship burns up, trash and all!

What fix-up strategies could you use to figure out the meaning of "conservation"?

Cleaning Up Space Trash

As long as humans continue to explore and use space, we will create trash. But nobody wants space to become a trash dump.

Governments of many countries are working to stop future space litter. Astronauts are now very careful not to create new space trash. New satellites will not be allowed in space unless they will be safe once they are no longer functioning.

What is the meaning of "functioning"? Explain the strategies you can use to figure out the meaning.

Scientists are working to control the current space trash problem. We now have a space traffic control system. Scientists monitor all large pieces of space junk. That way they know where big pieces of trash are, and spacecraft can avoid space pollution.

Maybe one day there will be missions to space to pick up junk. Who knows? You may grow up to become a "space trash collector"!

Think and Respond

Reflect and Write

- You and your partner took turns reading *Space Trash* aloud. Discuss the thoughts you had as you read.

- Choose two words you or your partner did not know in *Space Trash*. Write each word on an index card. Then, on the other sides of the cards write the strategies you used to figure out the meaning.

Syllables in Context

Search through *Space Trash* to find two words for each of the following categories: two syllables, three syllables, and four syllables. Make a list of your words. Draw lines between the syllables. Then compare your words with a partner's.

Turn and Talk

USE FIX-UP STRATEGIES: DECODING AND WORD ANALYSIS

Discuss with a partner what you have learned about using fix up strategies, such as decoding and word analysis.

- What does it mean to use decoding and word analysis?

Look at page 500. Which words do you find difficult to read? Discuss with a partner how to figure out the meanings of these words.

Critical Thinking

With a partner, brainstorm ideas about why disposing of trash is important. Then discuss answers to these questions.

- How is the problem with trash the same or different on Earth and in space?

- What do astronauts do to help prevent space trash?

- Do you think the problem of space trash will get better or worse? Explain.

Glossary

Using the Glossary

Like a dictionary, this glossary lists words in alphabetical order. Guide words at the top of each page show you the first and last word on the page. If a word has more than one syllable, the syllables are separated by a dark dot (•). Use the pronunciation key on the bottom of every other page.

Sample

The pronunciation guide shows how to say the word. The accent shows which syllable is stressed.

The part of speech shows how the word is often used.

Each word is broken into syllables.

nom•i•na•tion (näm´ ə nā´ shən) *n.* The act of suggesting someone for a job or honor. *Mia received the nomination for class president.*

The definition shows what the word means.

The example sentence includes the word in it.

Abbreviations: *adj.* adjective, *adv.* adverb, *conj.* conjunction, *interj.* interjection, *n.* noun, *prep.* preposition, *pron.* pronoun, *v.* verb

---

ab•so•lute•ly (ab´ sə lo͞ot´ lē) *adv.* Certainly. *I would absolutely love to go to the park with you.*

ac•com•plish•ment (ə käm´ plish mənt) *n.* The act of completing something successfully. *Finishing the race is a great accomplishment.*

al•low•ance (ə lou´ əns) *n.* An amount of money given out at regular times. *Erica gets an allowance of four dollars each week.*

a•lu•mi•num (ə lo͞o´ mə nəm) *n.* A light, silver-colored metal. *Soda cans are made of aluminum.*

a•re•na (ə rē´ nə) *n.* A closed-in area used for public events. *Ellen's favorite band performed at the arena.*

ax•is (ak´ sis) *n.* A straight line around which something turns. *Like other planets, Saturn turns on its axis.*

cam•paign (kam pān´) *n.* An organized plan to reach a goal. *Mr. Gonzales asked his good friend to help with his campaign for mayor.*

cap•tion (kap´ shən) *n.* A title or comment that goes with a photograph, illustration, or another kind of visual in a text. *The caption says the picture is of an oak tree.*

char•i•ty (chȧr´ i tē) *n.* A group that helps people in need. *Clarke's mom works for a charity that gives meals to the homeless.*

chem·i·cal (kem´ i kəl) *n.* A substance used or produced in chemistry. *Mixing one **chemical** with another can sometimes cause an explosion.*

clog (kläg) *v.* To block something. *Banana peels or potato skins may **clog** the kitchen sink.*

coil (koil) *v.* To wind into rings or loops. *Mom showed us how to **coil** a rope.*

col·lege (kä´ lij) *n.* A school where people can go after high school. *Uncle Richard teaches history at a **college**.*

col·o·nist (käl´ ə nist) *n.* A person who lives in a newly settled place. *Every year, my town celebrates the year the first **colonist** arrived.*

com·mer·cial (kə mʉr´ shəl) *n.* An advertisement on radio or television. *Many television programs run a **commercial** every fifteen minutes.*

con·fet·ti (kən fet´ ē) *n.* Small bits of brightly colored paper. *Everyone threw **confetti** at the parade.*

coun·cil (koun´ səl) *n.* A group of people elected or appointed to make decisions and laws. *My uncle was a member of the city **council**.*

cre·a·tiv·i·ty (krē´ ā tiv´ ə tē) *n.* Ideas for new things. *Prizes will be awarded for **creativity** in the school poster contest.*

crew (kro͞o) *n.* A team of people who work together to operate something. *Matt's father is a member of the highway work **crew**.*

crit·i·cis·m (kri´ tə siz´ əm) *n.* The act of judging something. *Simon offered his **criticism** to the singer.*

dain·ty (dān´ tē) *adj.* Delicate and attractive. *Samantha bought **dainty** teacups for her party.*

de·part·ment (dē pärt´ mənt) *n.* A separate section of business or government. *Mr. Kim works for the police **department**.*

dis·ap·point·ment (dis´ ə point´ mənt) *n.* A feeling of being let down. *The coach saw **disappointment** on the players' faces after they lost the game.*

dy·na·mite (dī´ nə mīt´) *n.* A powerful explosive. *The workers used **dynamite** to blast through the rock.*

end·less (end´ lis) *adj.* Without an end; extremely numerous. *The highway looked **endless**.*

fab·ric (fa´ brik) *n.* Cloth. *Mary made a dress out of yellow **fabric**.*

fund·rai·ser (fund´ rā´ zər) *n.* An event to raise money. *The hospital had a **fundraiser** for a new building.*

PRONUNCIATION KEY

a	add, map	oi	oil, boy	zh	vision, pleasure
ā	ace, rate	ou	pout, now	ə	the schwa, an
â(r)	care, air	o͝o	took, full		unstressed vowel
ä	palm, father	o͞o	pool, food		representing the
e	end, pet	u	up, done		sound spelled
ē	equal, tree	ʉ	her, sir,		*a* in *above*
i	it, give		burn, word		*e* in *sicken*
ī	ice, write	yo͞o	fuse, few		*i* in *possible*
o	odd, hot	z	zest, wise		*o* in *melon*
ō	open, so				*u* in *circus*
ô	order, jaw				

gang·way (gang′ wā′) *n.* A passageway to a ship. *Millie walked up the gangway to board the ship.*

gov·er·nor (guv′ ə nər) *n.* A person elected to be head of a state. *Mrs. Master's class went to Harrisburg to see where the governor works.*

grav·i·ty (gra′ vi tē) *n.* The force that pulls things down to Earth to prevent them from floating off into space. *Astronauts float in space because their spacecraft lacks gravity.*

green·house (grēn′ hous′) *n.* A glass room or building used to grow plants in a controlled environment. *We grew tomatoes in the greenhouse.*

groom (groom) *v.* To clean and maintain the appearance of something. *Kelly must groom her horse before the riding competition.*

hu·man·i·ty (hyoo man′ ə tē) *n.* All the people in the world. *Many people give gifts to charity for the good of humanity.*

in·stru·ment (in′ strə mənt) *n.* A tool used for a specific purpose. *A thermometer is an instrument used to measure temperature.*

in·tel·li·gent (in tel′ ə jənt) *adj.* Able to understand, think, and learn quickly. *Marie Curie was a very intelligent woman.*

in·vi·ta·tion (in′ və tā′ shən) *n.* A request for someone to come somewhere or do something. *Yolanda sent me an invitation to her picnic.*

mag·net·ic (mag net′ ik) *adj.* Relating to a piece of metal that attracts iron or steel. *A magnetic field is the area around a magnet.*

meas·ly (mēz′ lē) *adj.* A very small amount. *The measly amount of soap was not enough for Oliver to wash his hands.*

mesh (mesh) *n.* A material made from plastic or wire loosely woven together. *The porch screens are made of mesh.*

nom·i·na·tion (näm′ ə nā′ shən) *n.* The act of suggesting someone for a job or honor. *Mia received the nomination for class president.*

non·ex·is·tent (nän′ eg zis′ tənt) *adj.* Not living or being real; absent. *The pirate searched for clues to the location of the buried treasure and found them nonexistent.*

oath (ōth) *n.* A serious, formal statement making a promise. *The President of the United States takes an oath to uphold the laws of the country.*

opp·o·site (äp′ ə zit) *adj.* Completely different. *Turn around and go the opposite way.*

par·a·chute (pâr′ ə shoot′) *n.* A large piece of fabric that a person straps on to slow down a fall. *The soldier used a parachute to land safely after jumping out of the plane.*

plas·tic (plas′ tik) *n.* Man-made material molded and formed into different shapes and sizes. *Many small and large toys are made out of plastic.*

podium • wound

po·di·um (pō´ dē əm) *n.* A raised platform for a speaker or conductor. *At the assembly, the principal stood on the **podium** to speak to the school.*

po·lar (pō´ lər) *adj.* relating to the icy region at the North and South poles. *We saw penguins in their natural **polar** environment in the movie.*

pres·i·den·tial (pre´ zə den´ shəl) *adj.* Relating to the elected official in charge of a country or company. *The U.S. **presidential** office is in the White House.*

qual·i·ty (kwô´ lə tē) *n.* The nature or character of something. *Lucy's handmade quilt was very good **quality.***

rai·ling (rā´ lln̄g) *n.* A wooden or metal bar that acts as a fence or guard. *Tom painted the **railing** around the deck.*

re·ceipt (ri sēt´) *n.* Something written showing that money or goods have been accepted. *The store clerk gave Paco a **receipt.***

reg·is·ter (re´ jis tər) *v.* To enter someone's name in an official list. *When he turns 18, Peter can **register** to vote.*

rep·re·sen·ta·tive (rep´ ri zen´ tə tiv) *n.* A person who is chosen to act for others. *Sonia is a **representative** for her district.*

sap (sap) *n.* Liquid in a plant that carries water and food. *Maple trees produce a **sap** that can be used to make maple syrup or sugar.*

sculp·ture (skulp´ chər) *n.* Art that is carved or shaped out of wood, metal, clay, or another material. *Edgar Degas made a **sculpture** of a ballerina.*

shred (shred) *v.* To cut or tear into small strips. *To make papier-mâché, **shred** old newspapers as a first step.*

splurge (splɵrj) *v.* To spend a lot of money in a showy way. *People sometimes **splurge** on gifts.*

sports·man·ship (spôrts´ mən ship´) *n.* Fairness, respect, and kindness when playing a game. *The losing team showed good **sportsmanship** when they clapped for the winning team.*

waltzed (wôltsd) *v. past tense.* To move easily and smoothly as if dancing. *Henry **waltzed** into the party.*

weave (wēv) *v.* To make something by passing strips over and under one another. *The villagers **weave** baskets to sell at the marketplace.*

wound (wo͞ond) *n.* A cut in the skin. *The nurse put medicine and a bandage on his **wound.***

PRONUNCIATION KEY

a	add, map	oi	oil, boy	zh	vision, pleasure
ā	ace, rate	ou	pout, now	ə	the schwa, an
â(r)	care, air	o͝o	took, full		unstressed vowel
ä	palm, father	o͞o	pool, food		representing the
e	end, pet	u	up, done		sound spelled
ē	equal, tree	ɵ	her, sir,		a in *above*
i	it, give		burn, word		e in *sicken*
ī	ice, write	yo͞o	fuse, few		i in *possible*
o	odd, hot	z	zest, wise		o in *melon*
ō	open, so				u in *circus*
ô	order, jaw				

Acknowledgements

For permission to reprint copyrighted material, grateful acknowledgment is made to the following sources:

Chickens May Not Cross the Road and Other Crazy (But True) Laws by Kathi Linz, illustrated by Tony Griego. Text © 2002 by Kathi Linz. Illustrations © 2002 by Tony Griego. Reprinted by permission of Houghton Mifflin Company. All rights reserved.

from *Duck For President* by Doreen Cronin, Illustrated by Betsy Lewin. Text © 2004 by Doreen Cronin. Illustrations © 2004 by Betsy Lewin. Reprinted by permission of Simon and Schuster Books for Young Readers, an Imprint of Simon and Shchuster Children's Publishing Division. All rights reserved.

Floating Home by David Getz, illustrations by Michael Rex. Text © 1997 by David Getz. Illustrations © 1997 by Michael Rex. Reprinted by permission of Henry Holt and Company, LLC.

From Factory to You: How Paper Is Made by Isaac Asimov. Text TK.

Just a Dream by Chris Van Allsburg. Copyright © 1990 by Chris Van Allsburg. Reprinted by permission of Houghton Mifflin Company. All rights reserved.

Rachel: the Story of Rachel Carson by Amy Ehrlich, illustrated by Wendell Minor. Text © 2002 by Amy Ehrlich. Illustrations © 2002 by Wendell Minor. Used by permission of Harcourt, Inc.

My Rows and Piles of Coins by Tololwa Mollel, illustrated by E. B. Lewis. Text © 1999 by Tololwa M. Mollel. Illustrations © 1999 by E. B. Lewis. Reprinted by permission of Clarion Books, an imprint of Houghton Mifflin Company. All rights reserved.

The Solar System. Text TK.

Unit Opener Acknowledgements

P.256a Rivera, Diego (1886-1957)/© The Detroit Institute of Arts, USA, Gift of Edsel B. Ford/The Bridgeman Art Library International; p.318a Digital Image © The Museum of Modern Art/Licensed by SCALA/Art Resource, NY; p.380a The Newark Museum/Art Resource, NY; p.442a Digital Image (c) The Museum of Modern Art/Licensed by SCALA/Art Resource, NY.

Illustration Acknowledgements

P.266a Julie Olson/Wilkinson Studios; p.276a David Sheldon/Wilkinson Studios; p.277b David Sheldon/Wilkinson Studios; p.278a Mark Willenbrink/Wilkinson Studios; p.292b,c Deborah Huelsbergen/Wilkinson Studios; p.293c Deborah Huelsbergen/Wilkinson Studios; p.296a Tamara Petrosino/Wilkinson Studios; p.297a,b,c,d,a Tamara Petrosino/Wilkinson Studios; p.300a Carlton Salter/Wilkinson Studios; p.302a Carlton Salter/Wilkinson Studios; p.304a Carlton Salter/Wilkinson Studios; p.305d Carlton Salter/Wilkinson Studios; p.306a,b,c David Sheldon/Wilkinson Studios; p.308a Caroline Hu/Wilkinson Studios; p.310b Tom McKee/Wilkinson Studios; p.312d Michael DiGiorgio/Wilkinson Studios; p.313a Michael DiGiogio/Wilkinson Studios; p.328a Gervasio Benitez/Wilkinson Studios; p.329a Gervasio Benitez/Wilkinson Studios; p.332a Kristin Guerin/Wilkinson Studios; p.338d George Hamblin/Wilkinson Studios; p.341a George Hamblin/Wilkinson Studios; p.344a Carlos Aon/Wilkinson Studios; p.346a Carlos Aon/Wilkinson Studios; p.348a Carlos Aon/Wilkinson Studios; p.349b Carlos Aon/Wilkinson Studios; p.358d Jeff Grunewald/Wilkinson Studios; p.359d Jeff Grunewald/Wilkinson Studios; p.362a Joe Bucco/Wilkinson Studios; p.364a Joe Bucco/Wilkinson Studios; p.366a Joe Bucco/Wilkinson Studios; p.370a Adam Nickel/Wilkinson Studios; p.386a Maxx Baby/Wilkinson Studios; p.387b Maxx Baby/Wilkinson Studios; p.390a,a Paula Wendland-Zinngrabe/Wilkinson Studios; p.391a Paula Wendland-Zinngrabe/Wilkinson Studios; p.402a Jeff Hopkins/Wilkinson Studios; p.403b Jeff Hopkins/Wilkinson Studios; p.406a Burgandy Beam/Wilkinson Studios; p.407b Burgandy Beam/Wilkinson Studios; p.408a,b Burgandy Beam/Wilkinson Studios; p.409b Burgandy Beam/Wilkinson Studios; p.410a,b Burgandy Beam/Wilkinson Studios; p.411b Burgandy Beam/Wilkinson Studios; p.424a Luanne Marten/Wilkinson Studios; p.426a Luanne Marten/Wilkinson Studios; p.428a Luanne Marten/Wilkinson Studios; p.429b Luanne Marten/Wilkinson Studios; p.432a Scott Ritchie/Wilkinson Studios; p.436a Stephen Reed/Wilkinson Studios; p.438a Stephen Reed/Wilkinson Studios; p.440a Stephen Reed/Wilkinson Studios; p.441b Stephen Reed/Wilkinson Studios; p.448c Scott Ritchie/Wilkinson Studios; p.452b,d Burgandy Beam/Wilkinson Studios; p.453b,d Burgandy Beam/Wilkinson Studios; p.454a,c,c Kristin Guerin/Wilkinson Studios; p.464a Helle Urban/Wilkinson Studios; p.466a Dan Grant/Wilkinson Studios; p.467d Dan Grant/Wilkinson Studios; p.468a Julia Woolf/Wilkinson Studios; p.470a Julia Woolf/Wilkinson Studios; p.472a Julia Woolf/Wilkinson Studios; p.473a Julia Woolf/Wilkinson Studios; p.478b Bob Brugger/Wilkinson Studios; p.483b Michael DiGiorgio/Wilkinson Studios; p.484d,d Tamara Petrosino/Wilkinson Studios; p.485d Tamara Petrosino/Wilkinson Studios; p.486a Pam Anzalotti/Wilkinson Studios; p.488a Pam Anzalotti/Wilkinson Studios; p.490a Pam Anzalotti/Wilkinson Studios; p.491a Pam Anzalotti/Wilkinson Studios; p.494a Costa Alavezos/Wilkinson Studios; p.498a Jeff Grunewald/Wilkinson Studios; p.500a Jeff Grunewald/Wilkinson Studios; p.502a Jeff Grunewald/Wilkinson Studios.

Photography Acknowledgements

P.259a ©Courtsy of Wisconsin Historical Society 2nd use; p.262b ©Mikael Utterstr^m/Alamy; p.262c ©Robert Estall/Corbis; p.265c Element Photo Shoot; p.268a Element Photo Shoot; p.268b ©Courtesy of Sunshine Fresh Nevada LLC, North Las Vegas, NV.; p.268d ©Lisa Hubbard/PictureQuest; p.268d ©Scott Lanza/PictureQuest; p.269d ©Courtesy of Mt. Olive Pickle Company, Inc.; p.270d Element Photo Shoot; p.270b ©Photo courtesy of the National Association for the Self-Employed; p.271d Element Photo Shoot; p.272b Element Photo Shoot; p.272a ©Getty Images; p.274c,d

Element Photo Shoot; p.275b Element Photo Shoot; p.280a Element Photo Shoot; p.280b ©Associated Press, The Denver Post; p.280c ©Joseph Sohm, ChromoSohm Inc./Corbis; p.282a ©Johner Images/Getty Images; p.282b ©Getty Images; p.282d ©SSPL/The Image Works; p.283c Element Photo Shoot; p.283b ©Johner Images/Getty Images 2nd use; p.283d ©Corbis; p.284b ©Roger-Viollet/The Image Works; p.284b ©Courtesy of Jacquie Hatton/Keep Homestead Museum; p.284d ©Science Museum/SSPL/The Image Works; p.284c,d ©Courtesy of Jacquie Hatton/Keep Homestead Museum; p.285d ©Corbis; p.285b ©Geoff Brightling/Dorling Kindersley; p.286d Element Photo Shoot 2nd use; p.286c ©Courtsy of Wisconsin Historical Society; p.286d ©Bettmann/Corbis; p.292a Element Photo Shoot; p.295c Element Photo Shoot; p.298c Element PHoto Shoot; p.299d ©Paul Rapson/Alamy; p.312c ©Jim West/Alamy; p.314b ©Nevada Wier/Getty Images; p.314d ©Corbis; p.316d ©Bruce Coleman Inc./Alamy; p.324b ©1996 Corbis; Original image courtesy of NASA/Corbis; p.324d ©STScI/NASA/ASU/Hester/Ressmeyer/Corbis; p.327d Element Photo Shoot; p.330b Element Photo Shoot; p.330b ©Pekka Parviainen/Science Photo Library; p.334b ©M-SAT LTD/Science Photo Library; p.336b ©Space Telescope Science Institute/NASA/Photo Researchers, Inc.; p.338a ©Mauritius/SuperStock; p.338b ©Associated Press, AP; p.339a ©Photo Resource Hawaii/Alamy; p.340d ©Dr Fred Espenak/Science Photo Library; p.341b ©Roger Harris/Science Photo Library; p.342a ©John Chumack/Photo Researchers, Inc.; p.342d ©Matthias Kulka/Corbis; p.350a ©NASA/Roger Ressmeyer/Corbis; p.354d ©Original image courtesy of NASA/Corbis; p.357d Element Photo Shoot; p.358a ©Spirit-NASA/Getty Images; p.358b ©Reuters/ANU/Handout Reuters/Corbis; p.360a Element Photo Shoot; p.360b ©Ria Novosti/Photo Researchers, Inc.; p.360b ©Bettmann/Corbis; p.360d ©Marc Garanger/Corbis; p.367b ©Spirit-NASA/Getty Images; p.368a ©Courtesy of NASA; p.368b ©AFP/Getty Images; p.369c ©Courtesy of NASA; p.372a,c Element Photo Shoot; p.372d ©Franz-Marc Frei/Corbis; p.374a ©Imtek Imagineering/ Masterfile; p.375b Element Photo Shoot; p.375d ©Novosti/Topham/The Image Works; p.376d ©Douglas Kirkland/Corbis; p.377b Element Photo Shoot; p.377d ©Time Life Pictures/Getty Images; p.378a ©Corbis; p.382a ©Jose Luis Pelaez, Inc./Corbis 2nd use; p.389c Element Photo Shoot; p.392b ©Envision/Corbis; p.394b,b Element Photo Shoot; p.394b ©Courtesy of San Antonio; p.395a Element Photo Shoot; p.395d ©Ron Herndon/Herndon Panoramics; p.396b,c,d Element Photo Shoot 2nd use; p.397a,b Element Photo Shoot 3rd use; p.397c ©Andre Jenny/Alamy; p.398b,b Element Photo Shoot 4th use; p.398b ©Courtesy of San Antonio Parks and Recreation; p.398d ©William Manning/Corbis; p.400b ©Photo courtesy of The Salter House Museum; p.400d ©Getty Images; p.404b ©O'Brien Productions/Corbis; p.405d ©Chris Collins/Corbis; p.416b Element Photo Shoot; p.416a ©Chris Collins/Corbis; p.416c ©Bettmann/CORBIS; p.416d ©Jim Bourg/Reuters/Corbis; p.419d Element Photo Shoot; p.420c ©Associated Press, AP; p.420d ©Joseph Sohm; ChromoSohm Inc./Corbis; p.421c ©AFP/Getty Images; p.422a,c Element Photo Shoot; p.422d ©Bill Bachmann/Alamy; p.423e Element Photo Shoot; p.424b Element Photo Shoot; p.425b Element Photo Shoot; p.426b Element Photo Shoot; p.427b Element Photo Shoot; p.428b Element Photo Shoot; p.430c ©Benn Mitchell/Getty Images; p.430d ©Marc Serota/Reuters/Corbis; p.431c ©Chip East/Reuters/Corbis; p.434b ©Time Life Pictures/Getty Images; p.434d ©Bettmann/Corbis; p.435b ©Roger Ressmeyer/Corbis; p.448a Element Photo Shoot; p.449b ©William Manning/Corbis; p.451d Element Photo Shoot; p.456a,d Element Photo Shoot; p.456b ©Associated Press, AP; p.456d ©Bob Daemmrich/The Image Works; p.457b ©Bob Daemmrich/Photo Edit; p.458a Element Photo Shoot 2nd use; p.458d ©Stefano Paltera/Handout/Reuters/Corbis; p.459c ©Photo by Stefano Paltera/North American Solar Challenge; p.459b ©Courtesy of Nathanael Chang; p.460a Element Photo Shoot 3rd use; p.460c ©Associated Press, North American Solar Challenge; p.460d ©Associated Press, North American Solar Challenge; p.461d ©Associated Press, Topeka Capital Journal;" p.462b ©Danita Delimont/Alamy; p.462d ©Mark Tomalty/Masterfile/www.masterfile.com; p.462d ©Christine Robinson/Getty Images; p.462d ©blickwinkel/Alamy; p.466b Element Photo Shoot; p.474c ©Karl Weatherly/Corbis; p.481d Element Photo Shoot; p.482b Element Photo Shoot; p.482a ©Louie Psihoyos/Getty Images; p.483b Element Photo Shoot; p.484a Element Photo Shoot; p.492a Element Photo Shoot; p.492b ©Roger Bamber/Alamy; p.492d ©Danny Lehman/Corbis; p.493c ©Steven Poe/Alamy; p.496b ©Karl Weatherly/Corbis 2nd use; p.496d Element Photo Shoot 2nd use; p.496a ©Courtesy of Sea Fair Archives; p.496c ©Associated Press, AP; p.497d ©Silukstockimages.

Additional Photography by Alysta/Shutterstock; Angilla S./Shutterstock; Bedo/Dreamstime.com; Blend Images/Alamy; BLOOMimage/Getty Images Royalty Free; Corbis/Harcourt Index; Corbis/Telescope; Dennis MacDonald/Alamy; Digital Vision/ Naoki Okamoto/Getty Images; Elena Elisseeva/Shutterstock; Elke Dennis/Shutterstock; First Class Photos PTY LTD/Shutterstock; Freaksmg/Dreamstime.com; Getty Images Royalty Free/PhotoDisc/Getty Images; Getty Images Royalty Free/Telescope; Hans-Peter Merten/Getty Images Royalty Free; Ilya D. Gridnev/Shutterstock; image100/Alamy; Jenny Horne/shutterstock; Jeremy Woodhouse/Getty Images Royalty Free; Jonathan Feinstein/Shutterstock; Keeweeboy/Dreamstime.com; Laura Neal/Shutterstock; Library of Congress/Telescope; Lisa F. Young/istock.com; Mary E. McCabe/shutterstock; Najin/Shutterstock; NASA/Telescope; Photo Disc/Getty Images/Harcourt Index; PhotoDisc/Getty Images/Telescope; Photos.com Royalty Free/Telescope; Photos.com; Ronals Sherwood/Shutterstock; Royalty-Free/Corbis; Samantha Grandy/Shutterstock; Sean Haley /Istock.com; Stockdisc/Getty Images; StockTrek/Getty Images; Suzannah Skelton/istock.com; Tanya Constantine/Getty Images Royalty-free; Tootles/Dreamstime.com; WizData, inc./ Shutterstock.

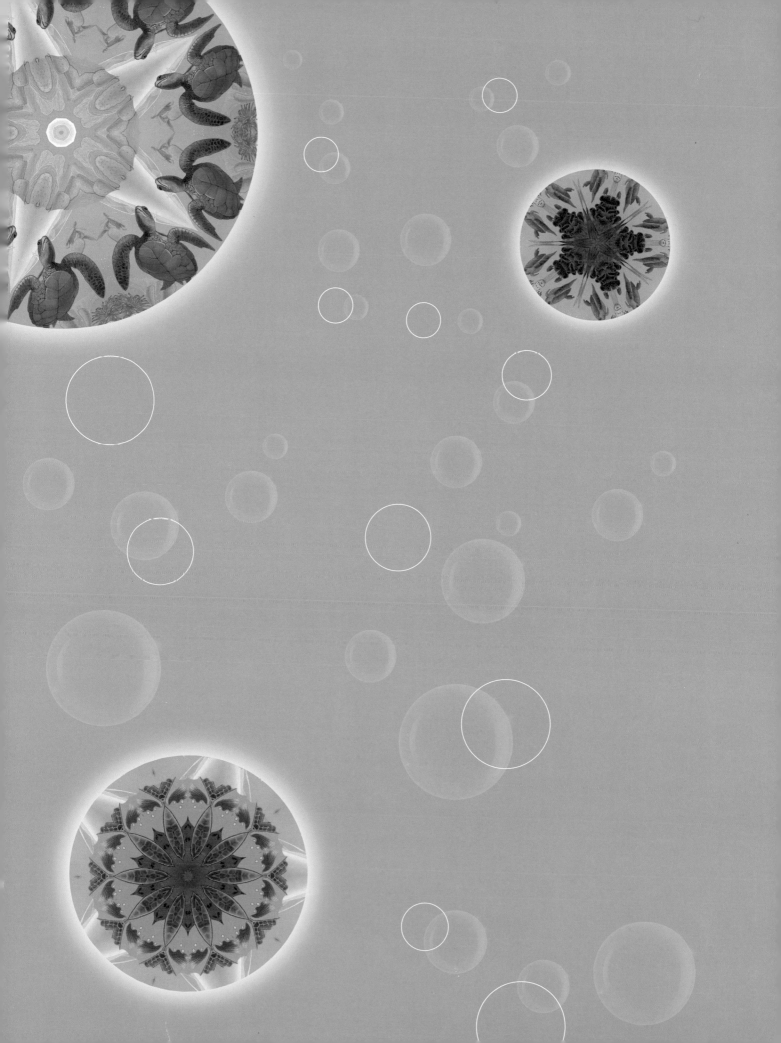

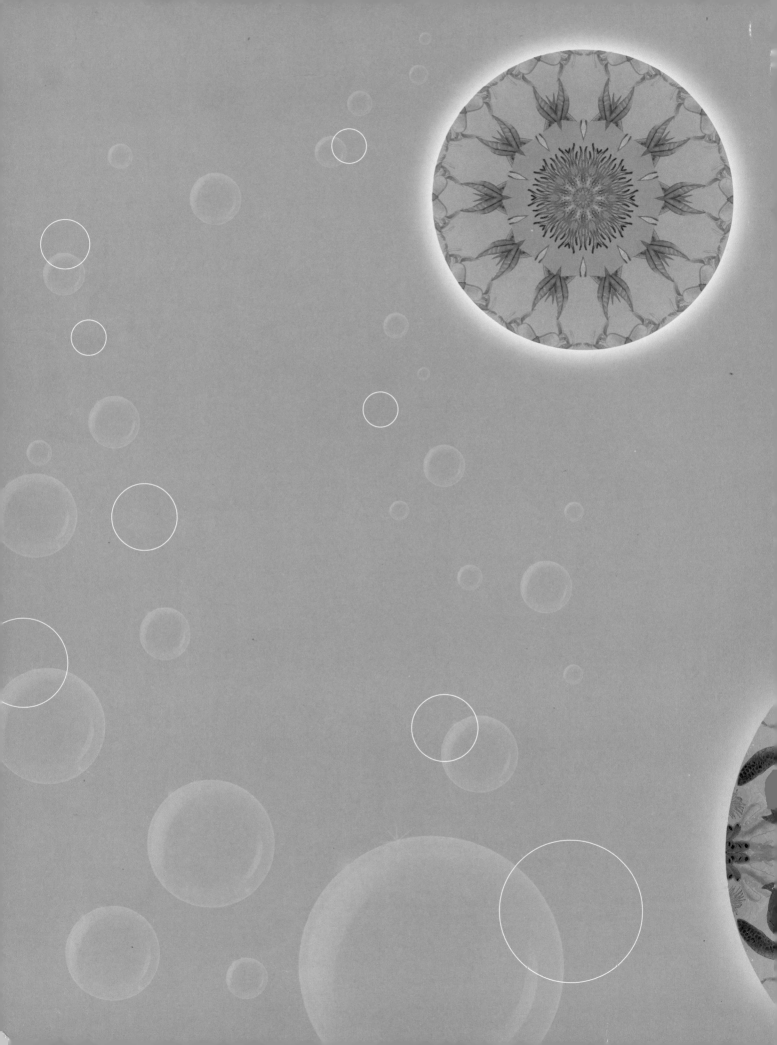